Almost Invisible

Almost
Invisible

Maureen Garvie

Groundwood Books
House of Anansi Press
Toronto Berkeley

Groundwood Books / House of Anansi Press
groundwoodbooks.com

We acknowledge for their financial support of our publishing program the Canada
Council for the Arts, the Ontario Arts Council and the Government of Canada.

 Canada Council Conseil des Arts
for the Arts du Canada

 ONTARIO ARTS COUNCIL
CONSEIL DES ARTS DE L'ONTARIO
an Ontario government agency
un organisme du gouvernement de l'Ontario

With the participation of the Government of Canada
Avec la participation du gouvernement du Canada | Canada

Library and Archives Canada Cataloguing in Publication
Garvie, Maureen, author
Almost invisible / Maureen Garvie.
Issued in print and electronic formats.
ISBN 978-1-77306-078-1 (hardcover).—ISBN 978-1-77306-079-8 (HTML).—
ISBN 978-1-77306-080-4 (Kindle)
I. Title.
PS8563.A6749A77 2018   C813'.6   C2017-907568-3
C2017-907569-1

Jacket design by Michael Solomon
Jacket art by Federica Bordoni

Printed and bound in Canada

 MIX
Paper from
responsible sources
FSC
www.fsc.org FSC® C016245

For Geeti Shafia, who was thirteen

1
Surprised

Maya

Back in May my friend Lily Larsen and I get dropped off at school really early for a drama rehearsal. It's so early the halls are dark and echoey, and the only sound besides our shoes squeaking on the floor is a buzzing from somewhere nearby.

Of course we have to stop in the washroom so Lily can check to make sure she's looking good. She pushes open the washroom door. And stops.

There's a girl in there, crouched under the hand dryer, drying her hair.

She whirls around and stares at us. Then she dashes to the basins, sweeps up her stuff and rushes past us into the hall.

Lily and I look at each other.

"What was THAT?"

"It was …" — it takes me a minute — "Jewel."

Jewel is in the other grade-seven class. We took science with them in the fall and Jewel was my lab partner a couple of times. She's been at our school since grade six. She's really quiet.

For a second I didn't recognize her, her hair dripping wet and looking at us like we were some kind of commando raid. I guess we startled her.

Lily goes to the mirror. On this particular day her hair is coming out the top of her head in two spiky bunches. She

11

has a fake tattoo of the Statue of Liberty on the side of her neck.

"Hey, Maya," she says. "Remember Jewel ran away?"

"Yeah. Then she came home again."

"Did she? Go home, I mean?"

"What do you mean?"

Lily fixes her eyeliner with her finger. "I think she's living in the school."

"Living in the school! She was just drying her hair. It's raining out."

"But what's she doing at school so early? It's not like she does drama or music." She leans down and sniffs at the basin. Points. "Smell. Here."

I lean down. Shampoo. "You think she was *washing* her hair?"

"Yeah. Here, at 7:12 in the morning."

"Maybe the hot water broke at her house. Maybe somebody else was in the shower."

"And also" — Lily pauses so she's sure she's got my attention — "she was making *breakfast*."

"Uh, breakfast?"

"You know when we went past the lunchroom? I smelled toast burning."

We go back out in the hall just as our friend Jerome comes up the stairs. Jerome is in the drama club too.

"What's up?" he says, and Lily tells him. And he goes, "Washing her hair in the girls' washroom? Maybe a bird pooped on her head." Then he tells Lily he can't come over to her place after school today to work on dolls because he's got track and field. "But tomorrow, okay? I got that Barbie to finish."

Other people are in the hall now, and he doesn't even keep his voice down. He just says "Barbie" in the same loud voice he says everything else in. Kids are always saying to me and Lily, "Aren't you a little old to play with Barbies?" So imagine what they say to Jerome — especially jerky boys like Trevor Slick and Ben Neva.

We're more into fashion dolls than Barbies now anyway. Once it used to be all Barbies — and American Girls — which was what me and Lily had in common when we first got to be friends. But we don't play with dolls now we're older. We repurpose them. We find them, like at yard sales and online, and fix them up — repaint their faces, reroot their hair, and dress them — and then Lily sells them online. Jerome does really good tattooing, especially on Kens and G.I. Joes. People also pay a lot for inked-up Barbies.

Anyway, getting back to Jewel, I don't see how wet hair and burnt toast add up to her living in the school. Also, when we have shared PE that morning with the other grade sevens, Jewel doesn't seem any different than usual. It's volleyball, and she's good at sports (like me), and she scores a couple of points.

So I don't see it coming when Lily says to me at lunch, "We need to follow Jewel after school."

"What for?"

"To see if she goes home, duh."

I have an orthodontist appointment, so that lets me out, but Lily texts her mother that she has to stay until four for extra choir. When school gets out, she and Jerome follow Jewel.

Jewel always walks home. Last year I'd be on the bus and I'd see her and her brother Anton walking home, but now that Anton is in high school, Jewel walks home on her own. Lily figures if Jewel's living in the school, she might not leave at all. Or she might just go a few blocks and circle back.

But she leaves, and she keeps on going.

"Maybe because she saw you stalking her," I say the next day. Lily and Jerome are hard to miss. Lily is five foot six with long jet-black hair. Jerome is five foot nine, blond with dark roots. (Whereas I am five two, curly brown hair.) And they're noisy, like a couple of crows.

"She never turned around, so I don't see how she could have known we were behind her," Jerome says. "It was like eight blocks to her house and she went right up to the door and went in."

So there goes Lily's theory.

"Is her house a dump?" I always figured Jewel was poor.

"Actually, no," says Jerome. "It's small but tasteful."

Which shows you shouldn't assume things. Except at lunch Lily says to me, "You know the house Jewel went to? That's not her house." Lily got the idea to look up the address, and the name of the people who live there is Owen or something. Jewel's last name is Morante.

"She might be in foster care," I say. "Remember, she ran away."

"Twice," Lily reminds me.

Right. First time was last year, in grade six. The vice-principal, Mr. Admunson, came to our class and asked if anybody'd seen Jewel Morante. Next day, though, Jewel was back. Her eyes were swollen like she'd been really crying. The day after, though, she seemed normal.

So when Mr. Admunson came to our class at the end of March and asked if anybody'd seen Jewel, we figured she'd show up in a day or two. She didn't, though. She was actually gone quite a long time. The day she did show up, she looked thin, with dark circles under her eyes, and she smelled like smoke. Not like cigarette smoke or burnt toast. More like a campfire. Lily and I went up to her at lunch and asked if she was okay and she said yes. She didn't look at us, just concentrated on her soup like she didn't want to spill any. We could see she didn't want to talk.

She was on her own like usual. She didn't have any friends that I knew of. It's not like there was anything wrong with her, though. I mean, she didn't have body odor or anything, and I would have known because she was my lab partner. She was average weight, not obese or anorexic. I never heard anything about her throwing up in the bathroom. And she was okay looking. Ordinary dark hair with no style. The opposite of Lily. Everything Lily wears is a style statement. Lily has a little red tartan dress with a tube top she wears with kitten heels and fishnet tights and fingerless gloves. My mother says it's in very bad taste for someone her age and people might get the wrong idea about her, but Lily always looks amazing. If I wore what Lily wears, everybody would just laugh.

But Jewel? Jeans and hoodies. Almost invisible. Which I guess is also a style statement.

It was only seeing her drying her hair in the washroom that made us wonder what was going on with her. Jewel was not somebody we ordinarily thought much about. Her brother Anton was a lot more interesting (at least Lily thought so), more outgoing and better looking. The only reason I noticed Jewel at all was when she first came to our school, some kids got in trouble for picking on her. They'd walk into her and say, "Oh, *sorry.* Didn't see you." They were harassing her because she was so quiet it was a bit creepy. They were trying to get her to react.

She'd just mumble, "It's okay." It got to be a thing, until the school principal, Ms. Harpell, gave us the bullying talk at assembly. She didn't say Jewel's name but everybody knew who it was about. I felt kind of bad, and mostly people quit walking into her. Except for jerks like Ben Neva and Trevor Slick, but those guys are reptiles.

Jewel's brother Anton wasn't quiet like her. He was only at our school for grade eight, but he made lots of friends. He was a soccer star. When he was on the team, our school won the inter-school tournament for the first time in its entire history. Probably the last time too.

Jewel is nothing like her brother. In science last fall the teacher was always trying to get her to participate. She never put her hand up, but he kept asking her questions. She'd look down at her desk until he gave up. Occasionally, though, she'd say something, and it could be really smart. When we were lab partners, she did all the stuff I didn't understand. It was mostly because of her that we got really good marks.

I don't know anything about her family, although I heard they came from Quebec. In French, she has a Quebec accent. She doesn't have any accent in English, though.

Jerome thinks maybe she's so quiet because of her religion. "Maybe she's Mormon or Muslim or Jehovah's Witness and it could be against their religion for girls to talk to people." Except it can't be against their religion for boys, because Anton always talked to anybody he wanted, including girls.

Jerome follows Jewel home a few more times and says she never goes anywhere except the same house. We decide Lily was crazy thinking Jewel could be living in the school. Lily keeps checking the girls' washroom, but she never catches Jewel washing her hair in the sink again, or her underwear or anything. We stop thinking about her.

Well, I do notice how she's always by herself when she's outside school too, like on the street or at the store. In our neighborhood, that's unusual. Hardly anybody I know is a free ranger. Any time I go out, even on my bike, Mom or Dad say, "Take Claire with you." Like they think that if I'm on the street on my own for five minutes without my ten-year-old sister, somebody is going to grab me and stuff me in a car and take me somewhere and cut me into pieces.

I don't mean to joke about it, because that happens. Not a lot, but you do hear about it — some girl disappears and everybody's looking for her and it's all over Facebook. It happens to boys too, I guess, but more often it seems like it's a girl. And her mom and dad go on TV and say they're sure she's alive, because they'd know if she was dead, they'd *feel* it. And then she turns up dead.

I can't imagine how bad I would feel if that happened to Claire. If it happened to me. But like how many people do you know it's happened to? Probably none, right? At least I really, truly, sincerely, totally hope not. I know bad things happen to kids that mostly you don't hear about. Parents knock their kids around or lock them in the attic. Or the guy next door abuses them for years and nobody notices. Other kids pick on them until they get so desperate they jump off a bridge.

And when the news comes out, everybody is so shocked.

2
Running

Jewel

My sister Charmaine ran away, so that's where I got the idea. But where I ran to, that was my idea, from the school trip we went on to the conservation area in grade six. Mom never even knew I went on it. If I asked her, she would've said *We haven't got that kind of money to throw around you stay home and look after Nico.* So I just signed her name on the permission sheet like usual and paid the twenty dollars out of my babysitting money. After I turned thirteen and did the babysitting course, Mrs. Owen gave me a raise to five dollars an hour, and I never told Mom anything about that either. I gave her the usual and kept the extra back.

I used to keep money in a hole in the box springs of my bed until I found Charmaine's bank card. She must have gone in a real hurry, leaving it in her coat pocket like that. I already knew her PIN because she used to let me take out money for her when I was little. I thought she might have got out money from it after she ran away, but she didn't. Well, she didn't have her card, did she? She didn't have much money in there anyways, and I didn't think she'd mind me using her card to put mine in. Charmaine never minded anything I did.

I wasn't worried about getting caught going on that school trip because Dad or Mom never called the school about anything. I almost didn't go, that day started out so bad. Mom threw a fit about Nico spilling his juice and he started screaming and it went on from there. I got him out of her way and cleaned him up and changed him and sat him in front of the TV, and it seemed like she calmed down, so I thought it would be okay to still go. I was afraid the bus might have gone, but it was still at the school. I even got a seat by the window and after I sat there awhile my stomach started coming out of knots.

Our class went to the conservation area one time before, back in the winter. We were supposed to bring our skates then, and mine were too small, but they had snowshoes that anybody could use for free and a big fire in the fireplace to warm up after. I liked it there then, but this trip was even better, the sun shining and little leaves just coming out.

The man who was showing us around — Gordon, he said to call him — showed us a stuffed dead animal in a case and asked if anybody knew what it was. It looked like a fox to me, only its fur wasn't red and the head didn't look right. Trevor Slick said, "A wolverine?" and Ben Neva said, "A hyena?" and everybody laughed.

Gordon said actually wolverine wasn't too far off as it was in the same family. He said it was called a fisher, and we might see a live one if we were lucky. He said a couple of days before, some visitors saw a mother fisher carrying her babies across the parking lot. She walked across with one in her mouth and left it somewhere down near the lake and then came back for another.

"You've probably heard that fishers kill cats and dogs," Gordon said. "But fishers aren't evil or mean. They're just wild animals. Only people are evil or mean." The animal in the glass case looked mean, but it probably wasn't very happy about being killed and stuffed. I wished I could have seen the live mother with the babies.

When we went outside, Gordon took us to a hole in the ground with a fence around it and a sign that said it used to be a mica mine and Keep Out. One of the boys crawled under the fence to go down the hole and get some mica. Right after he got yelled at, I stepped on a rock, and when I looked down I saw it glinting. I thought it might be gold, but Ms. Abrams came up behind me and said, "Hey, everyone, Jewel found some mica!"

Because that was what it was, a lump of mica. Gordon took it and showed everybody how they used to peel layers off it. He said people used mica for glass back when they didn't have any glass. That's what they had that mine for. Gordon gave me a chunk he split off because it was me that found it, and he kept the rest.

Maya, a girl from the other grade-six class — I didn't know her then, it was before she was my lab partner — she came up to me and asked, "Can I have a little piece off of it?"

"You can have it all," I said. Because if I took it home, Mom might ask me where I got it. Or she'd throw it away unless I hid it, and what would be the point of that?

Maya said, "Cool! Thanks! But you should keep some. You found it." She peeled off some thin layers for me and her and her friends. They all held theirs up and looked through them, so I did too. It was sort of like glass, like Gordon said, but it made everything shadowy and orange.

It was good finding something those girls thought was cool. It would have been even better if I saw the mother fisher with her babies, but it was a good day anyway. Well, not at the start, but it got better.

On the bus home, halfway out to the highway we had to stop for Marcia Harding to throw up. Marcia throws up every time we go somewhere on a bus. We stopped beside a lake and while we were waiting I looked at it out the window through the mica. The lake came up almost to the road, and across on the other shore was a log cabin with a weeping willow and a dock for a boat and real ducks sitting on the lawn. Along its front the cabin had a covered porch with flowerpots down the steps. Looking at it through the mica made it all golden, and I thought, who wouldn't be happy living there?

I knew exactly what it would be like inside. The kitchen would have a table for eating at in front of the window, with daisies in a jar. The living room would have a fireplace and a red couch with pillows. And the bedrooms would have bunk beds like the boys have at the Owens' where I babysit. I'd have the top bunk, with lots of quilts and pillows.

That all came to me in a flash. I don't know how, because the only cabin or cottage I ever went to was later, in the summer with the Owens, just for the day. And that cottage was like a regular house, except at a lake. They brought me along to make sure Danny and Liam didn't drown while the adults were talking. Liam was only two then.

When Ms. Abrams got Marcia Harding back on the bus and we drove off and I couldn't see the cabin anymore, I felt like I was leaving a friend behind. All the rest of the way back to school, everybody was yelling and shouting and the boy behind me kept kicking the back of my seat. My dad would have turned around and ripped his face off, but I didn't say anything. I just imagined being at that log cabin, lovely and peaceful all on my own, or with maybe a cat.

Once we had a cat, an orange stripey kitten called Tiger. Nico loved it. Charmaine and me had to keep taking it away from him because he squeezed it too hard. Then the dog killed it and that was sad. And if I had a cat at the cabin, it would be sad not to bring Nico, but he would be just too hard to look after there. Also, I wouldn't have money from babysitting to buy all the things we'd need, and cat food.

Anyway, it was all only an idea I had in my mind. It wasn't real.

That was back in the spring. When summer came and the holidays started, there wasn't much to do so I'd sit on the back step and imagine being at the log cabin. I'd imagine rocking in a chair on the front porch or putting my feet in the water at the end of the dock. If I was babysitting, sometimes I looked through Mrs. Owen's decorating magazines to find nice things for the cabin. One time I saw some dishes I really liked, with chickens running around the edges and cups like chicken bottoms for boiled eggs. I asked Mrs.

Owen if I could borrow the magazine to copy the page at Staples, and she said, "Just tear it out and take it, Jewel." She can be bossy about stuff like stacking the dishwasher or making sure the boys brush their teeth for two whole minutes, but other times she can be nice.

And when school started up again in the fall, any time bad things happened at home, like if Mom whacked me or she hit Nico with the iron cord, I'd just imagine I was at my cabin curled up on the couch with a fire in the fireplace. Once I went on Google Maps in the resource room at school to figure out where the lake actually was. I worked out that it was called Otter Lake and I looked up how far it was, and it said twenty kilometers from our school. I thought there might be a bus there, but it said the bus only went to the 401 highway. I'd have to walk the rest of the way. It said it was four and a half hours to walk from the 401 to the conservation area. I figured I could walk for that long, twenty kilometers. If I started at ten, I'd be there by two-thirty in the afternoon.

It was only something I imagined. I wasn't planning to run away there or anything. Well, sometimes I thought about running away, but I knew I'd have to have a good plan if I did. Because one time before I ran away and that was a bad idea, because then I didn't have any plan at all.

The first time I ran away, I just went to Belleville. That was after Charmaine went and me and Nico were missing her so much. Nobody said anything about where she went, and when I asked when she was coming back, Mom said, "When hell freezes over," and Dad told me to shut the fuggup.

At the end of February, Charmaine was gone four months. On garbage night I was collecting the kitchen trash to put outside and I looked in the bag and saw a piece of envelope all crumpled and ripped up. I got a shock, because it had my name on it. It was printed in capital letters, but it looked like my sister's printing.

I never heard about any letter coming from her. They never told me it came, and it was me she sent it to.

One day she was there like always and the next morning she was gone. When she didn't come home after school, I looked in her room and all her clothes were still there, even her coat. Her phone and her bank card were in the pocket, and I felt glad when I saw that. She wouldn't have left them if she wasn't coming back. I took them and hid them so Mom and Dad wouldn't get them.

Only, she never did come back, and I never knew they heard a single word from her.

So there I was standing with the trash bag in one hand and the piece of envelope with my name on it in the other.

Mom was watching a movie in the living room and Dad was out. I got the rubber gloves and dumped the garbage out on some old flyers. Fast as I could, I pawed through everything — stinky chicken skin, soggy Kleenexes, old coffee filters and tea bags. I thought they might have tore up the letter to me and put it in the garbage too but I couldn't find any letter.

I found more of the envelope, though. It was ripped in four, but I got the pieces. I smoothed them out on the counter. No return address. Charmaine's name wasn't on it either. I could see something stamped on the corner that seemed like it said *Belleville*. That's a town that's not too far from here.

I put the pieces in my pants pocket and went right through the garbage again. Two-for-one pizza flyers and cards asking did we want to sell our house or get a new furnace. Also some of the cardboard squares Mom cuts off of her cigarette packages for writing notes on, like *Doctors, 10:30*, or *Get milk*.

One square was folded in half. It had bacon fat on it, so I almost didn't unfold it.

But I did. Mom wrote on it: *320 Birch St #205*.

"What the hell is going on in there?" Mom shouted at me from the living room.

"I'm doing the garbage." I cleaned up the floor fast and put the pieces of envelope in the hidey-hole under my bed.

Next day at recess I went to the resource center and did a search on Birch Street. No Birch Street in Kingston. But in Belleville there was, and there was a 320 Birch Street too.

The day after that, instead of going to school, I got the bus to Belleville. It's ninety kilometers. I was afraid you couldn't go on the bus by yourself if you were only twelve, and I didn't want to call up and ask because if they said you couldn't, they'd be more likely to be thinking about it when I showed up. So I wrote a note from my mother saying I was going to my aunt's in Belleville and I put Charmaine's old cellphone for my mother's phone number. I wrote in the letter that my aunt was meeting me at the bus station.

When I got out to the terminal, there was a long line to buy tickets. I went to the washroom and put on a lot of eyeliner so I looked more like Ariana Grande and not like myself at all. I got my money and permission letter ready and went in line. I was really nervous.

I got up to the glass wall with the hole to talk and put your money through, and the man on the other side said to me, "Where to?" and I said, "Belleville." He said, "One way or round trip?" and I said, "Round trip." And he said, "Student? That'll be $42.45." I expected it would be a lot, but I had my babysitting money. I pushed sixty dollars through the hole and he pushed the ticket and the change back, and he was already talking to the lady behind me.

That's all there was to it. I didn't have to use the note I wrote. He didn't even really look at me.

I went out to the bus with all the other people and gave my ticket to the driver and climbed on. Now that I wasn't so scared about getting stopped, I started getting excited about seeing Charmaine. I'd been mad at her for a long time that she just left and forgot about me and Nico. But she didn't forget after all. She wrote me a letter, only I didn't know. I was so happy. I was thinking of asking her to let me stay with her in Belleville.

I had the taped-up envelope in my pack and Mom's cardboard with the Birch Street address on it. I knew from looking it up it wasn't too far to walk. It was a cold windy day, but I only had to go four blocks. I found the apartment no trouble and rang the buzzer for the number on the card, 205.

Nothing happened, so I kept buzzing, and after a while I could see a woman coming down the hall. She was carrying a baby and my heart started thumping.

That's why she disappeared. She was afraid of what would happen if Mom and Dad found out she was having a baby.

And then she opened the door and it wasn't her.

She was older than Charmaine, heavier with a flat, tired face, not like Charmaine at all. She kind of glared at me.

"Was that you was buzzing? The intercom isn't working. What do you want?"

"I've come to see my sister," I said. "Charmaine Morante. She lives here."

"No she don't." She shifted the baby to her other hip. He was a big baby with a head like a beach ball and he kept smiling and holding out his hands to me. Babies like me. "I've lived here three months and I never met any Charmaine. There's only four apartments, and downstairs is mine and some old guy's, and upstairs is two old ladies."

I showed her the envelope I stuck together with Scotch tape.

"What's her last name again?" she said. "I might of seen some mail for her."

"Morante."

She shook her head. "Nothing ever came for that name that I saw."

But then I said Charmaine got married and she might have a different name. I didn't think of that before I said it. She had a boyfriend, Sam, and they might have got married. I never saw Sam after she ran away either.

"Let's have a look at the envelope."

I held it out for her to see but I didn't let go. She must have thought it was funny, dirty bits of paper all taped up.

"Come on, I'm not going to take it. I just want to look at the postmark."

So I let her have it and she held it up close to her face. "No wonder. Before I moved here."

I knew it was from Belleville but I never knew the date was on it too. She looked away from the envelope at me.

"You come from Kingston? Like that's you it's addressed to? How'd you get here? Shouldn't you be at school?"

"My brother gave me a ride."

"How old are you?"

"Fourteen. I have to go meet him now. Thanks anyway."

I waved goodbye to the baby and smiled, even though I was going to start crying as soon as I got out the door. I walked away fast.

The next bus back to Kingston wasn't for two hours and I couldn't think of what else to do except walk back to the bus station and hang around. I saw there was a Tim Hortons up the street, so I went and got tea and sat down at a table. An old man two tables down reading a newspaper said hello to me. He was doing the crossword and he asked me if I knew a five-letter word for a raptor. I didn't even know what a raptor was but he kept asking stuff like that. After a while I thought I might ask him something back, how I could find out if my sister still lived around here. I told him I was waiting for my brother to meet me and he was somewhere looking for her too.

I'm good at lies. Once I say them, sometimes they sound more like the truth than what's real. I even had a picture in my head of Anton going up and down the streets, knocking on doors and asking for Charmaine. I nearly expected him to walk in.

"I'd look in the phone book," the old guy said. "Roy," he called across to the guy at the counter, "you got a phone book? This young lady needs to look up a number."

Roy was a short guy with no hair but he still wore a hairnet like they have to. He got me a phone book. I didn't really expect there'd be any C. Morante in it, and there wasn't. Maybe she married Sam like I said. I didn't know his last name.

"You could ask at city hall," Roy said.

"They don't know nothing there except collecting parking tickets and taxes," the old man said.

"The utilities," said Roy. "She'd have hydro. They'd have her address."

"They don't give out that kind of information."

"You never know." Roy said city hall was just down the street, so I drank my tea and started to go. He crooked his finger at me, called me over.

"Might want to go to the washroom and fix your face."

In the washroom mirror, I had streaks of black running down my face. I looked like a clown. I forgot I'd been crying.

When I came out again, a policeman was at the counter picking out a box of donuts. I headed toward the door fast, but the old guy called out to the policeman, "Hey there, Frank, this young lady could use some help."

I would have just ran out the door but the policeman told me to sit down and he'd be over soon as he got his order. I should have ran. He came over and asked me my name and where I lived. I told him my name was Alice, which was the first thing that came into my head, and I told him about trying to find my sister. He asked me Charmaine's last name.

"Morante, but she might be married now," I said. "I think she has a different name." I showed him Mom's cardboard with the address. "I think that's where she lived."

He took it by one edge so he didn't have to touch the garbage stains on it. I showed him the envelope with Belleville stamped on it too. He said I should come out and sit in the police car while he made some calls. If he had any luck, he'd drive me to Charmaine's place. I got in the back seat.

The minute I got in, I knew it would all be bad. I should have ran.

He stood outside with his face turned away from me and talked on his phone.

33

When he got in again, he said, "No luck, Jewel." So it turned out he'd tricked me. They all tricked me, the old guy and Roy too.

"I'm not Jewel, I'm Alice," I said.

And he said, "The only Morantes in Kingston don't know any Alice, but they got a Jewel that sounds a lot like you."

"What about Charmaine?" I said. "You said you'd look for her."

"Why are you running away to find your sister? Things not good at home?"

"You said you'd try to find her. You tricked me. You lied." He didn't like me saying that. He wasn't interested in Charmaine. He drove me halfway back to Kingston and met up with another police car and they drove me home.

Dad lit into me as soon as they left, threw me against the wall and slapped me around. I tried to tell him I never said anything to anybody about him or Charmaine or nothing. I kept my mouth shut like they told us to.

It didn't make any difference. I still got it. Mom just kept screaming, "Don't hit her on the face!"

So I knew if I ever ran away again, I had to work it all out before I went so I didn't make any more stupid mistakes. I had to have a very good plan. I couldn't afford to get caught again.

Now that I was a year older and didn't look so much like a kid, I figured it would be easier to run away. Also, I had $250 in the bank from babysitting.

I started collecting stuff for running away. Mostly I got it at the dollar store, like a little flashlight and batteries, candles and matches, other things I figured I might need. If I went to that cabin by the lake. I kept it all in a hole in the box springs under the mattress, same place I kept Charmaine's bank card and her cell. It used to be Charmaine's bed and I found the hiding place when I got moved into her room after she left so I could mind Nico. The hole didn't have anything in it, though. Her cell was in her coat pocket. Mom and Dad never knew she had a phone, so they don't know I have it now. The Owens are the only ones who know. Mrs. Owen texts me on it if she needs to change arrangements for babysitting, like she used to do with Charmaine. That way she never has to talk to Mom and Dad. Charmaine was the sitter first, but when she went away, Mrs. Owen asked me. She knew I wasn't old enough, but she was desperate. She told me how to pay for the phone with cards you get at the grocery store. I already knew the phone password because it's the same as Charmaine's PIN.

I also started buying food to take when I went. It had to be stuff that wouldn't go stale and it had to be small enough to keep in the hiding place and light to carry in my pack. Like granola bars and crackers, and different-flavored oatmeal cereal you add hot water to. And ramen noodles, which are cheap, three for a dollar sometimes. You can even eat them without cooking and they don't taste that bad. I learned that from Anton. I figured I could buy apples and cheese once I left, and water.

Except none of it was really a plan, because how could I really go? What would happen to Nico without me there? It was all just stuff I was doing to make myself feel better. Like it would make me safe somehow.

So when I did run away, it was almost the same as that time before. Something happened, and I just went.

The night before I ran away, I got woke up by Mom and Dad bringing people back from the bar. I could smell cigarettes and I heard the fridge opening and shutting. Glass broke and somebody swore. People kept coming down the hall, bumping against the walls, going in the bathroom and the toilet flushing. I put the pillow over my head and tried to get back to sleep because next day was a school day. I wished I could lock my door, but Dad busted the lock off back when it was Charmaine's room.

I must have gone to asleep, though, because all of a sudden there's a hand over my mouth and horrible breath in my face. Someone's on top of me, pushing up my pajama top, pulling at my pajama bottoms. Whiskers scraping my cheek, grunting in my ear, "Don't worry, sweetheart, it's just Eddie. Eddie'll take care of you."

I couldn't move. I couldn't breathe. He was squashing all the air out of me. I struggled as hard as I could and my arm knocked the lamp on the floor. That woke Nico up and he started screaming. Eddie swore and twisted around so his hand came off my mouth, and when I started screaming too, he hit me in the face. Nico was shrieking bloody murder and then the light came on and a bunch of people were standing in the doorway.

Dad pushed through yelling, "What the fugginghell's going on, Eddie? What the hell you doing to my daughter? Get out of my kids' room, you filthy bugger!" He hauled Eddie off me and shoved him out in the hall.

All the time Nico kept on screaming.

"Shut it!" Dad roared and gave him a wallop across the ear, and for once Nico stopped.

Everybody stood there for a minute staring at me and then they all backed out in the hall and shut the door. Nico started up crying again, only whimpering this time. Nobody could hear him anyway with all the noise outside, Dad yelling and Mom screeching, car doors slamming and engines starting up, tires squealing.

Then it was all quiet. After a while I turned on the light and got a clean T-shirt and pajama bottoms and threw the other ones in the closet. I was shaking so much I could hardly stand up. I had red marks on my breast where Eddie squeezed it. Creepy, shitty old Eddie, Dad's friend. He was always hanging around, tickling me, rumpling my hair and stuff. I hoped Dad threw him out on the sidewalk and smashed his stinking face in.

The sheets on my bed stunk like him, so I pulled them off and threw them in the closet too. Nico was standing up holding on the bars of his crib, his face all tears and snot.

"There, there, Nico, quit your crying or Dad'll come back in and smack you again."

I found his dummy for him and stuck it in his mouth, hauled him out of his cot. He was heavy, he's almost five. His hair needed washing and his diaper was wet. I didn't care. He saved me. He shouldn't need a diaper, he was through all that, but when things get bad, he forgets.

I got a dry diaper on him and brought him in my bed under the quilt and patted his skinny back.

"You saved us from the bad man, Nico," I told him. "Be quiet or he'll hear you and come back."

Nico doesn't like cuddling but this time he let me. After a while he stopped crying and I stopped shivering.

And all this time my mother didn't even come out of the kitchen. I could hear her in there laughing.

Next morning I was making my tea in the microwave and waiting for Anton to get out of the shower when she walked in.

"Put the coffee on, would you?" she said. She sat down at the table with a groan and watched me. I could see her looking at the bruise on my cheek.

Anton rushed in the kitchen and started banging cupboard doors. "Shit, Mom, there's nothing to eat again!"

She sniffed and puffed on her cigarette. "That lot last night ate everything. Like a bunch of frigging locusts."

"I gotta *eat*, Mom. I got basketball practice."

"Ask your sister. She's got money."

I shook my head. "I gave it all to you, Mom." She swore and told Anton to get her purse out of her room. She gave him a ten to buy something at McDonald's, and he left. He didn't say anything to me about last night either, but he might have slept right through everything.

Mom lit another cigarette from the end of the one she was smoking and pointed with it at my face. "That'll learn you."

Like it was my fault what Eddie did. Same as happened to Charmaine, and it was never ever Charmaine's fault.

I heard Nico yelling upstairs so I went to get him up. On the way past the living room, I looked in and there was Eddie passed out on the couch.

They knew what he did and they let him stay.

I stood there a minute watching him snore and scratch his ass. Then I went upstairs and got Nico dressed and took him to the kitchen and put him in his chair with toast and his cup. I was shaking so much I spilled his milk on the counter.

Then I went back to the bedroom and lifted the mattress and the box springs and stuffed everything from the hidey-hole into my pack. I slammed the front door behind me and when I got to the end of the block, I turned the other way from school. No way I was going there, feeling dirty and horrible, sitting next to those shitty kids with their nice clothes and their nice houses and their nice moms and dads.

I walked downtown and got sixty dollars out of the bank machine. Then I got the Children's Aid number on my cell from 411 and left a message they should check up on Nico because his parents didn't look after him so well. I called Mrs. Owen and left a voice message for her too. She would have already left for work, but that was the idea. I didn't want to talk to her. I said, *I'm really sorry for the short notice about not being able to babysit after school for a while but I have to go to Montreal with my parents because my dad's mum is dying.*

That was a laugh. I had no idea if she was still alive or not.

I found out from the bus kiosk the number of the bus to the city limits. It went right past our street, but I kept my head turned away from the window and nobody much was out that early anyway. We passed a McDonald's and a Subway and a bunch of gas stations and the bus stopped at a hotel before the 401.

The driver looked in his rear-view mirror and said to me, "This is as far as I go." I said thanks and got off and went up the street like I knew where I was heading until I heard the bus drive away. Then I turned around and walked to the overpass and kept going. I knew from the Google map the road went to the conservation area.

It was cold, near freezing but bright, and I stopped being cold. Every step I went, I felt a tiny bit better. A bit, not a lot. I was worried what would happen to Nico without me. I hoped the CAS would pay attention to what I said on the phone and go check up on him.

When I came to a gas station that had a convenience store, I went in. I didn't buy much food because it was expensive and also heavy to carry. They didn't have much fresh anyway, but I got apples and oranges and cheese curd and yogurt. I sneaked some sugar packets and plastic spoons from where people fix their coffee.

I started eating an apple as soon as I got back outside because I never had any breakfast except some tea. When I bit into the apple, my front teeth were sore. I could feel the bruise on my cheek when I chewed.

It was supposed to take four and a half hours to walk to the lake. When I read that online, it didn't seem so long. Like I left at eight o'clock, so I should get there after lunch.

It seemed long now, though. Sometimes the cars going past honked at me. I didn't look, just went straight on like I had somewhere I was going.

At least I was warm enough. It hadn't snowed for a while, being the end of March, but I was wearing my parka because it was still cold. When my feet got tired I took a rest on a rock in the ditch where people in cars couldn't see me. I kept thinking about the cabin and how I was getting closer every minute. I kept thinking about the bunk bed with those fluffy pillows and quilts.

It was a lot more than two hours before I got to the sign for the turnoff to the conservation area. More like three hours, and that was supposed to be the halfway point. After that, the road wound around and around, up and down. The mud sucking at my shoes slowed me down more.

I started worrying somebody might be in my cabin. I never thought about that before. I mean, it didn't feel like spring yet, and the cabin seemed like someplace people would only come to in the summertime, but I didn't know that for sure.

A car came up behind, so I got way off to the side. I kept walking, didn't look around, but the car pulled even with me and slowed right down.

Somebody called, "You need a ride?" A woman. She had her window rolled down.

"No, thanks," I said back. "I'm not allowed to take rides. I'm not going much farther."

"Where you headed?"

I didn't say anything, just shrugged and kept walking. She kept driving along beside.

"Come on, honey, it's a long ways in. I tell my kids not to take rides from strangers, but you look like you could use a lift. Sure, I'm a stranger, but I'm a mother too."

That's no guarantee of anything.

"No, but thanks anyway." I smiled like everything was great.

She drove on then, but slow, like she still might stop and back up. Her brake lights kept going on. I looked for somewhere to get off the road, but there wasn't a driveway or nothing.

Finally she went around the corner. I let out my breath. I wished I could have got in that car with her, I was so tired, and my feet were so sore, but getting out again would have been a problem. She'd have wanted to know where I was going.

Next time I looked at my watch, I'd been walking almost five hours and I knew I still wasn't anywhere near. Whoever on Google said four and a half hours total couldn't have tried it. Probably those people don't get out much, ha ha. Maybe it seemed longer because the road had so many turns and ups and down. Google Maps might only tell you how far it is straight and level. I ate another apple with most of the cheese curds.

This road didn't have much traffic. In summer it was probably busier. A couple of pickup trucks came up behind me but they didn't slow down, and two cars passed me going the other way. I was limping now because my feet were blistered, but if I heard a car coming, I walked like I was fine.

It seemed like the temperature was going down. I could see big patches of snow in the woods. Also, wild animals lived in those woods, like those fishers that killed cats and dogs. At the conservation area they said there were coyotes too. And it was going to be dark in a couple of hours. I just had to keep putting one foot ahead of the other, even when it seemed like I couldn't take one more step. I didn't stop to rest anymore because I was afraid I might not be able to start again.

And then I came around a corner and there was the lake and my cabin!

It was exactly like I remembered — perfect. The sun was low and the light was all golden, like looking through the mica that time. I limped faster to the turnoff. I was terrified somebody'd be at the cabin, but I didn't see any car in the drive or any lights on. So far, so good.

The back door was locked. I walked around to the front, right up the porch steps. That door was locked too. But I expected that. Who'd be stupid enough to leave a nice place like that unlocked? Except all the times I imagined coming here, being locked out wasn't a problem. Mrs. Owen keeps her key over the back door where anybody could find it in five minutes. I was sure I'd figure out where the key was kept, or I could just break a window and fix it later.

Only thing was, all the windows were boarded up. I never pictured that.

I felt along the door frame and on top of all the window frames I could reach, but no key. Another place that people leave keys is under a flowerpot, but all the pots I saw on the porch steps last summer were gone. I thought the key might have been kept on a nail in the shed, but that was locked too.

I was getting frantic, stumbling around looking in the mailbox, turning over rocks, all the time my feet just about killing me.

And then I tripped over a tree root and fell on my face. That really hurt. It was already sore and now my nose was bleeding, and my chin was scraped.

I gave up on the cabin. A little ways down the road was another cottage, so I hobbled along to there. I kept listening for cars, but not a single live person was around except me. I tried the door of that place. Locked again. No key on the door frame, no key under the mat.

I was feeling like crying now because I didn't know what to do next. I didn't have a plan for this happening. The state my feet were in, I couldn't walk back home. I couldn't even walk out to the highway.

I limped on down the road. Three more cottages, all locked tight. I started talking to myself out loud. *I'll be eaten by bears. All they'll find is my bones.*

My shoes felt squishy. I figured it was blood, and now I had a twisted ankle from when I fell. Maybe I could crawl under a cottage and get through the night there. I found one basement door with a crummy little padlock and I picked up a rock and bashed at it. Nothing happened. I hit it again, harder, and screamed. I bashed my hand instead of the lock.

I was moaning and sucking my bleeding knuckles and staggering around. *That's it, I'll just die. I'll just freeze to death.* And then, way along the lake in the woods, I got a glimpse of one last place.

It was like the witch's cottage in Hansel and Gretel, except it wasn't made of any gingerbread. The closer I got to it, the worse it looked. It was creepy looking and run-down, the roof all green with moss. But it was my only hope.

And then I walked past a monster seven feet tall, staring through the trees at me with glowing yellow eyes. I screamed and screamed, except part of me knew while I was doing it that it wasn't really a monster, it couldn't be. I finally made myself look and it wasn't alive. It was only a big stuffed head somebody nailed to a tree, a moose head with great big horns, antlers, whatever. It wasn't in good shape, with the fur hanging off it in strips and the white skull showing through.

I took a deep breath and kept on going. I was almost there.

Slipping and sliding over an old crust of snowdrift up against the door, I grabbed the rusty knob. It turned.

The front door swung inward with a groan.

I waited for something to come rushing out and tear my head off.

Nothing happened. I couldn't hear a sound.

Inside was completely black, a black hole. Last thing I wanted was to go in. But my choice was between what was inside and being eaten by the wolves and bears and freezing to death outside.

I felt along the wall for a light switch. My fingers found one, and I clicked it on. It didn't work.

I found my flashlight in my pack and shone it around. I could see a heap of stuff dumped in the middle of the room. Beer boxes, firewood. Lumpy black garbage bags — probably body parts in them. The windows were covered with curtains and blankets. I stepped in and shut the door behind me.

Limping around the pile, I made myself look in all the other rooms with my flashlight. Kitchen, bathroom, two bedrooms. All bitter cold and silent as a tomb. I was so scared I thought I would throw up. Any second I expected to see some dead thing hanging from the ceiling.

I could hardly stand up, I was so tired. The second bedroom I came to, I pushed everything off the bed onto the floor except for an old sleeping bag and then I lay down and pulled it over me. The stuffing was coming out and it smelled like oil, but I pulled it over me, parka and all. I didn't even take my shoes off. I felt in my pack for an apple and gnawed on it. I was in a bitter cold, filthy place. But I was inside. That was something.

I thought the noise of my teeth chattering would keep me awake, but it didn't.

I woke up in pitch dark, thrashing, yelling. Flopping around, shrieking, all tangled up in the smelly sleeping bag.

Charmaine is screaming and I hit him with the broom handle across the back he lets her go and turns around roaring grabs me yanks me by the hair Mom shrieking don't leave a mark on her she'll go to the CAS.

No she won't or I'll kill her and that retard of a kid too. You hear me? You hear me? If you run away I'll find you we can find you no matter where you hide and you'll wish you'd never been born.

Yanking my hair until it comes out in his hand. You hear me? You hear me?

Yes I hear you.

Then I remembered where I was.

Alone. No Dad. No Mom. No Eddie.

It didn't make me feel much better.

I cried for a while. I felt so miserable and scared and sore. The bruise on my face ached and my bashed hand and scraped chin were throbbing. I tried to take my shoes off but my feet had blown up like balloons. One ankle was all swollen, the one I twisted when I fell. Maybe I broke it.

Maybe I'd get gangrene and they'd have to cut my leg off. Maybe I'd just die.

I cried about lost Charmaine and poor little Nico. It wasn't Nico's fault he was like he was. I wondered if the CAS came to the house after I phoned. I wondered if the police were looking for me. I hoped that woman who tried to give me a ride didn't call them. I hoped I'd go back to sleep and never wake up.

Only I was too freaked out to get back to sleep. Also, I had to pee. I felt for my little flashlight in my pocket and hobbled to the bathroom with it. The toilet didn't flush but I peed in it anyway. The cupboard over the sink had some stuff in it: an old box of Band-Aids. It took a while to get my shoes off because my hands were so cold. I had to peel my socks off the blisters on my heels, and that started the bleeding again.

Finally I got the Band-Aids on and went back to bed and crawled under the sleeping bag. It was a long time before I stopped shivering. I kept the flashlight on. It was so freaking silent, like my ears were stuffed with cotton, like I was in a coffin. I started saying crazy things out loud. *Peanutbutter bloodpoisoning floorpolish eenymeenymineyMyLittlePony thesecretofwhiterteeth.* To prove I was still alive.

And next thing I knew, a bit of light was showing through the curtain.

I lifted up the edge and looked out. It was a different world from last night. Everything had turned white. Fluffy flakes were falling like duck feathers, slow and soft, piling up on the branches. Snow was coming down so thick that

I couldn't see the other side of the bay. Yesterday it was almost spring and now it was back to winter.

I was snowed in.

Scary. But magical.

My watch said eight o'clock. I must have slept twelve hours at least. I couldn't get my feet in my shoes, but I got more socks out of my pack and put those on.

I pulled the blankets off the big window in the main room so I could see out. Then I thought I shouldn't have done that, because people could look in and see I was there. But who was going to be coming all the way down here in all the snow? What I should really be worried about was freezing to death. I could see my breath.

I tried turning on the stove. Didn't work, no electricity, duh. But the main room had a stove that burned wood, which I figured out because the wood for it was in a heap right next to it, with some old newspapers in a box. So that was a no-brainer, except I didn't know how to get it burning. I shoved some wood in the stove and some newspaper and lit it with the matches I brought in my pack. It caught right away and made a lovely heat, but then the paper burned up and the fire went out again. The wood wouldn't burn, only the paper, and every time I opened the door on the front to put in more paper, smoke came out. The room got so smoky I could hardly see.

The stove was so full of ashes it didn't leave much room for wood. I finally had the idea of emptying them out. I scraped them into an empty beer box with a piece of wood and lit more newspaper again. After a while I got some wood to keep on burning. I was really proud of myself about it until I turned around and saw the beer box with the ashes was on fire.

Even with blisters and a sprained ankle you can move fast to keep yourself from burning to death. I got to the door about three seconds before the bottom of the box dropped out and threw it as far as I could. The flames flared up until nothing was left but a gray mess and a steaming hole in the snow.

My hands were black, but at least they weren't burnt. And when I got back inside, the wood in the stove was still going.

Next thing was to eat. I got some ramen out of my pack, but there was no water to boil it in. I tried chewing the noodles raw, but I really wanted something hot. Then I had an idea. Snow makes water! I got pots out of the cupboard, and the snow outside was a foot deep so I could fill them. I put the pots of snow on the woodstove, and pretty soon I had water.

I made water out of snow! I was a genius! I even figured out I could flush the toilet if I put a bucket of water down it. It took a while to make that much, though. A whole pot of snow only made a little bit.

While I waited for the ramen water to boil, I dragged a chair from the kitchen and sat right close to the stove. That was nice, except my socks were sticking to the floor. Stuff was spilled on it, probably beer from all the bottles that were on the counter and the tables and the floor. I never saw such a pigsty. Mouse droppings everywhere too. I couldn't believe people would leave a place in such a mess. People that were probably not that poor either. I mean, they couldn't be too poor if they had a cottage, even a creepy one.

At least at our house it was clean. Every Saturday Mom had me scrub the kitchen floor. Like Cinderella, ha ha.

I started putting beer bottles in the empty boxes. I filled a box of two-fours before the water boiled. I meant to only eat half the ramen and save the rest for later, but I ended up eating it all. Afterwards I felt tired so I shut the door on the woodstove and went and lay down in the bedroom. I was still in a horrible place, but at least I wasn't so hungry or cold anymore. At least I didn't have to worry about Dad or Eddie or anybody else. Only Nico. And Charmaine.

When I woke up, it was still snowing and the wood in the stove was almost burnt away. It heated the place nice. The wood box was almost empty but there was lots more dumped on the living-room floor.

I kept on wondering what kind of people would live like this. Or maybe it was somebody that broke in here like me. Maybe they were criminals that brought the stuff they stole here to hide it before they moved it. I hoped they weren't coming back.

I got up my nerve to look in the garbage bags, and it wasn't body parts in them after all, just old boots and extension cords. Scrunched-up bags from Canadian Tire with nails and fishing tackle. None of it was any use to me, except a dirty pair of Crocs. They were men's, but they stayed on okay with the extra socks.

The living room had a couple of shelves of old magazines, mostly motorcycle ones, not for choppers like Dad's but dirt bikes and the bright shiny ones he calls Jap crap. Also, a really rude old magazine called *Playboy*. It was all pictures of girls with no clothes on or just their underwear. Any men in it were dressed. The girls looked happy enough, but probably they were getting paid for having their pictures taken like that. One girl reminded me of Charmaine, but when I looked closer it wasn't that much like her, just the hair. Charmaine is more real-looking. Most of those girls in the magazine looked like dolls.

I was starting to have an idea of the people who came here. Creepy guys, for sure, with those magazines and all the beer bottles and the moose head hanging on the tree. But I was also thinking they might not be really bad. The stuff in the Canadian Tire bags was just ordinary. I didn't find needles or guns like that. Maybe those guys were like Anton, just allowed to get away with whatever they wanted and nobody made them do stuff or told them how to do it properly.

I was thinking this place must have belonged to a family once because some of the stuff must have been nice when it was new. The wallpaper in the kitchen had chickens and ducks on it. It was dirty now, and the ducks had holes in them where somebody used them for target practice. Also, I found a couple of kids' books on the shelves and some other books that didn't seem like guys would read them. One book was about a girl who went to Australia to seek her fortune and married a mean farmer. From the picture on the cover, a girl with long hair running through the woods, I figured no guy would read that.

I always liked reading. Charmaine too. Charmaine loved books. We went to Goodwill to get them, sometimes really cheap. When I was little, I only liked ones with animals.

Some with bears called Berenstains were really funny, and I liked that they were a family. They weren't much like real bears, though.

One book we had was about a toad. I liked it because it was so small it could fit in my hand. Also, it was in French and English both, like the toad *hops around / sautille ici et là*. The toad finds a marshmallow in the woods, *une guimauve en pleine nature sauvage*. I don't know how there would be a marshmallow in the woods, but there was.

That's the only book that Nico likes. "Eesee ayla," he says. "Eesee ayla." *Ici et là*. That's all the French he knows. Even though he's half French like me. I got sick of reading it to him, but I was glad there was something he liked. I wish I read it to him more.

I got sad thinking about how different Nico is from Danny and Liam. When we read books, Liam sits on my lap and puts his arm around my neck. He's just little, only four. Nico's almost five and he doesn't like cuddling. He won't ever sit for long. Something's the matter with him. He might be autistic. Mom doesn't like him because he's not cute and happy. Neither am I. Charmaine was, but look how much good it did her.

I took the book about the girl who went to Australia and read by the woodstove. I read that book all afternoon. It did a good job of keeping my mind off my feet and what I was going to do next. I liked it being about Australia, with kangaroos and koala bears and all that. Also it was good where the girl helped the farmer save his farm from a forest fire, even though he was mean. He turned out to be not that mean after all. Also, he was rich and good-looking, which helped.

It started getting dark again and it was hard to read. I lit one candle and I could have lit more, but then I'd run out fast. I didn't want to use up all my flashlight batteries either. The only other light was from the woodstove, if I left the door open. That made things cozy, and the sound of it snapping and humming was sort of company, but I couldn't read by it very well. So that didn't leave me anything to do but think.

Thinking's okay for making plans or for school but not for the other stuff, the stuff that comes in your head whether you want it there or not. Charmaine taught me how to stop the bad thoughts. She called it "Stop-Thought." You put up a big red stop sign in your mind, and if the bad thoughts keep coming, you make the sign bigger and bigger until all you can see is STOP. Until you can't see the bad thoughts around it. Once the sign is holding the bad thoughts back, you go in your mind in the other direction, far away from them to a good place. Like I used to go to my cabin all the time. Except now I was at my cabin for real, and look how that turned out.

Stop-Thought wasn't working too good for me right now. I felt terrible for leaving Nico. What was going to happen to him with both me and Charmaine gone? Nobody else would look after him or clean him up or keep him out of Mom and Dad's way. Dad said if he hit him, he'd end up killing him. Anton could look after him, but he wouldn't. Anton doesn't have a clue. Well, about sports, sure, and he does okay at school. He isn't stupid. Just, it's all about Anton. Mom thinks the sun shines out of his ass.

Dad used to hit Anton but not in a while. Anton's good at keeping out of his way. I am too. It was Charmaine that always got the worst. It seemed like Dad liked her for being pretty, but that didn't stop him hitting her. Sometimes he pinched her tit hard and laughed when she yelled. Mom said, "Cut that crap out, Leon," but it was more like she didn't like him giving Charmaine the attention. She called Charmaine a slut. But Charmaine wasn't any slut.

When she went, not knowing what happened to her made me half-crazy. I listened all the time for clues but I never heard a peep. I was afraid something bad happened to her, so after I found that envelope, I felt better. Maybe I shouldn't have. Stop-Thought.

I wondered if the CAS checked up on Nico after I called. I thought about seeing if my phone worked here and calling them again. It was Charmaine's cell and nobody except Mrs. Owen knew I had it, but maybe the CAS could tell where I was calling from. So I didn't call.

I got back in bed and pulled the sleeping bag over my head and it was only six o'clock. I couldn't put myself to sleep imagining running away to stay at my dream place in the woods because I'd run away and it wasn't like in my dream. So I just cried for a while until I fell asleep.

When I woke up it was morning and it was still snowing. I thought, good. The more snow, the less chance that people would come around. The drift outside the door was so high I could hardly get out. I got more snow and boiled water for oatmeal cereal, apple-cinnamon flavor. My blisters were still bad but my ankle wasn't broken because I could stand on it. I only had a few pages of the Australia book left so I finished it and started another. I didn't like that one as much. It had murders, which weren't that good to think about, being where I was.

So for something else to do, I started cleaning.

I put the rest of the beer bottles in boxes and piled them all in the back room. I dragged all the garbage bags from the living room in there too. That room already had a lot of junk in it, and after a while I couldn't get much more in.

All the wood that was dumped on the floor of the main room I stacked against the wall. Most pieces were so heavy I could only carry two at a time. It took ages but that was okay. I wasn't going anywhere. The carpet was covered in sawdust, so I went looking for a broom. I found one with bristles all bent one way, but I did the best I could with it. Nothing I could do about the stains.

I heated more snow for water and washed down the table and counter with an old towel. The door frames were so black in places I thought they were burnt, but it turned out to be only dirt. I even washed the gross kitchen floor. I do know how to clean. That's one thing that kept me in Mom's good books.

I was looking in the cupboards for cleaning supplies when a miracle happened. Way at the back I saw something that looked like a can. I stuck my arm in and got it. Beans. I stared at it like it was gold. I stuck my arm in again and got another can. More beans! After that I just pulled everything out onto the floor. Three empty bottles of dish soap, a can of Drano — and two cans of tuna and a can of spaghetti! All the food was pushed right to the back. They must have forgot they had it. That got me going through all the other cupboards, but the only other food I found was a canister with rice with dead bugs in it, and two packages of microwave popcorn.

I wasn't going to steal any of it. I'm not a thief. I still had my oatmeal and ramen. Except I was getting sick of ramen, and I couldn't stop thinking about those cans. The label on the beans said *Made with real maple syrup*, and that sounded really good. I still had nearly fifty dollars left from my babysitting money. I could leave some to pay for what I used. Also, I'd cleaned up the place a lot, so they owed me for that. I should get a reward.

Those beans tasted totally great.

I kept on cleaning the next day too because it was something to do. All the junk in the living room I piled in the middle of the carpet, and then I dragged the furniture out from the walls so I could sweep up all the leaves and dirt and beer caps and mouse poop. Then I pushed the furniture to where I wanted and put everything away, on the shelves or somewhere. I had to do it all really slow, but I had the time. My ankle was still bad and I couldn't stop thinking about food, so I boiled a lot of water and drank that. I didn't want to go through my food supply too fast.

To keep from thinking too much, I made up movies in my mind. One was of me going in the convenience store I went in on the way here and putting up a notice saying I was a qualified babysitter. And then somebody up the road from here with a baby hiring me. I say I'm sixteen and they believe me because I have on my Ariana Grande eye makeup. And the mother and father go out to work and they say, "We couldn't manage without you, Alice." Maybe they suspect I'm not as old as I say, but they don't want to think about it because I keep the kids off their back. Like Mr. and Mrs. Owen.

One time I saw Mrs. Owen looking at me and she said, "Is everything okay with you, Jewel? Everything okay at home? You're not being bullied at school?" Because I guess I looked sad or something.

"I'm good," I said. "I just got my period." Which I don't yet, but that's what Charmaine used to say, and it worked, because Mrs. Owen left me alone after that.

By the afternoon the snow stopped for good. The sun came out for the first time since I got here. Pillows of snow started falling off the trees, plopping on the roof. When I went outside, crows were cawing, and little birds I didn't know the names of were chirping and squeaking. It was noisy!

The snow was glittery and sparkly against the blue, blue sky, and the sun shining through the trees made stripey bands out on the ice. I went back inside and sat in the nice clean living room in front of the window to figure out what I should do next. Stay here forever. That's what I wanted to do. Only I was going to run out of food a long time before then.

I could walk back to that convenience store and buy food. But sooner or later the people who owned this place would show up. They might call the police, unless they were criminals and didn't want to get caught themselves. They might let me stay and live with them, like Snow White and the Seven Dwarfs, them going off in the morning and me having supper ready when they came home from work. Ha ha. More likely they'd kick me out and start messing the place up again. Or worse. They might be like Eddie.

Anyway, I couldn't hide my whole life, because what about Nico? He wouldn't have much chance with me gone too. And how would I ever find Charmaine? The police never even looked for her after she went. Somebody must have reported she went missing because they came around to our house, but Mom and Dad just told them she ran off with her boyfriend. Dad said she took off with guys all the time, which was a lie, she never did. She only had the one boyfriend, Sam. I know she was in Belleville from what was stamped on that envelope. That policeman that said he was going to look for her, he took the envelope off me and never gave it back. If he kept it, he should have found her, but it seemed like he didn't even try.

Now I didn't have the envelope or Charmaine either.

My other choice was to go home.

Don't you try running away like that bitch your sister. I'll fix you like I fixed her. I'll kill you. You'll wish you were never born.

So going home wasn't a choice.

Next morning I woke up so early it wasn't even light. The woodstove was still warm, so I built up the fire and got the logs snapping away. And all of a sudden I decided what I really, really wanted was a bath.

I worked out it was five days since I had a proper wash. My hair was practically crawling. Even the morning I ran away, I didn't have a shower because Anton used up the hot water.

I heated four big pots on the woodstove, the most I could fit on top. I put more logs in and opened the door so it was roaring. By the time the water was hot, the place felt like a tropical paradise.

I laid out a clean T-shirt and underwear and socks over the back of a chair. I washed out the dishpan with snow and set it on the floor next to the stove. Then I half-filled it with hot water cooled down with more snow so I didn't scald myself. Then I took off all my clothes and stepped into my tiny tub. It was just was big enough to get both feet in.

The one piece of soap I had left had teeth marks from where the mice had been eating it. I soaped myself all over and used dish detergent for my hair. My sprained ankle had gone black and there was still a yellow bruise on my breast, like a hand. In a little mirror hanging on the wall I caught sight of myself: a pale, skinny ghost with hollows for eyes.

I trickled a pot of warm water over my head and then the next one. It felt lovely. I kept doing it until the pots of water were all gone.

And then I heard a noise outside.

I grabbed my dirty T-shirt and wrapped it around me and crouched down in the dishpan. My back was to the door and I was too petrified to turn around. Heavy footsteps came crashing up to the door like someone in an awful hurry.

They found me.

Whoever was out there could still see me through the window in the door. The door wasn't locked. I shut my eyes, waiting for it to crash open. Whimpering, waiting.

I held my breath, my eyes tight shut.

Nothing happened. No knock. No door opening.

And then I heard footsteps running away!

It's Anton. He's gone to tell them he found me.

For the longest time I couldn't move. My arms tight around myself. The water in the dishpan getting cold.

Finally I made myself look over my shoulder. Nobody was there. Nobody was at the door looking in. Maybe they hadn't seen me after all.

I stood up and stepped out of the dishpan, trembling so hard I almost fell over. Part of it was I was cold and part of it was I was half out of my mind.

I dried myself with my old T-shirt, put on my clean clothes. Once I was dressed and stopped shivering, I felt a bit braver. Of course it wasn't Anton, or Dad or Eddie or any of them. How could it be? Not a single person in the whole world except me knew I was here.

Except would whoever was there have seen smoke coming out the chimney? Why didn't they knock or come in?

I looked out the window for tracks in the snow to see how many feet had made them. I couldn't see much so I opened the door a crack.

And I saw tracks all right. But they weren't human ones.

Up the hill, in the misty light, were deer. Just standing, not moving a bit, like spirits of the forest, velvety gold against the white snow. They were looking right at me and I looked back at them and we all stayed perfectly still. For ages.

I never ever saw a live deer before. There were five, two big ones and three small. So beautiful.

I said, really softly, "Hi."

I used a quiet voice, but it still broke the spell. They swirled around, their tails going up in the air like white flags, and away they went, leaping over the hill out of sight.

Magic.

By then the sun was coming up, and pretty soon it was pouring in the windows. After a while it warmed up the place so much I hardly needed the woodstove.

I put away the dishpan and swept the floor again, and as I was putting the broom away in the storeroom, I happened to notice a big metal box hanging on the wall. I don't know why I noticed it now. I climbed over the boxes and the garbage bags I'd piled in there and opened the door on the box, and inside was a long row of switches and a big switch. I pushed some of the switches up and down and nothing happened.

I pushed the big switch and the lights went on.

The lights went on! And for five days I'd been sitting in the dark like a moron.

I ran around turning on every single light. I tried the stove and the microwave, and those worked too. I turned on the kitchen tap and no water came out, but that didn't matter. I could get water from melting snow. I must have been mental not to think of turning the power on before. I guess I must have figured the people didn't pay their hydro and the power got cut off. Or maybe I thought at a cottage you only got power in the summer. I don't know what I was thinking.

By that time it was so nice outside I went out and walked around a bit. I saw other footprints in the snow besides the deer, I didn't know what kind. Not very big, so maybe squirrels and rabbits. And I saw birds. Crows — I know what crows are — and one was a woodpecker because it was pecking wood. And friendly little birds with little black hats — they came quite close — and gray birds and squawky big blue birds. Even red birds. I didn't know there'd be so many kinds.

I wished Nico could see them. Maybe someday Nico and I could have a cottage, and I could show him birds.

I went back inside and cleaned some more and started reading another old book, a mystery with a tough detective. That got me through the day. When it was dark, I walked through the snow a little ways up the road to see how much light showed through the windows now I had electricity.

I just about died. The whole place was lit up like a Christmas tree. I ran back and pulled all the curtains closed and turned off all the lights except one. I hung the blankets over the windows again. One light was plenty to read by. I read until I fell asleep. It was a lot better than lying awake in the dark thinking.

Being on my own it was hard not to listen to the things in my head. Things popped into it for no reason. Some were good. Like Mr. Bronson writing on my story "Best Family Holiday Ever" that I had a good imagination. True, because it was all lies. Maya saying to me in science I was smart. Liam and Danny making me macaroni pictures at daycare. One time Anton took me to a movie. Mom said he had to for some reason, but he bought me popcorn and he didn't need to do that.

I remembered the time we went to visit my gran — real Gran, Mom's mother that lives in Quebec City, not the made-up sick gran that's the excuse for missing school. Nico wasn't born yet and I was little. Me and Charmaine slept in the same bed.

Real Gran was skinny with gray braids she wound around her head. She took them down in the morning to braid them over and then she pinned them up again. She did it before she put in her teeth. She had horrible horny toenails she told us was from banging her toes on the railway ties walking to school. Anton said she was really a zombie, but she was just old. She gave us chocolates that were so stale they turned white.

Gran never took much notice of me, but one night in the car coming home from somewhere, I fell asleep and Gran put her arm around me. She was so bony it felt like leaning against a board, but I didn't move away. I thought she might love me.

My food was running really low. I waded through the snow in the woods looking for something to eat, only I didn't have a clue what to be looking for. In school we read about the Iroquois making tea out of stuff they found, like cedar tips. I thought they might have boiled the fungus that was growing on some of trees, but I was afraid it might be poison.

I don't know how the Iroquois could live when it was winter. Mostly all I could see in the woods was trees and rocks. Animals, I guess. I saw more tracks in the snow, and a couple of squirrels way up in the trees, but I wouldn't know how to catch them. There was mice in the cabin, because I heard them at night and they left poop on the counter. I might be able to catch a mouse in a trap, but no way I could eat it.

I wasn't sure if the green bits I got off trees were cedar, but whatever they were, they worked okay for tea. They didn't make me sick. They weren't food, though, even if I boiled them for a long time.

The tenth day the pain in my stomach woke me up in the dark and I couldn't get back to sleep. All I could think of was food. I was getting pretty used to that, only now it was a lot worse, and I'd run out of ways to do anything about it.

The only thing left to eat in the whole place was a package of microwave popcorn. I tried before to pop it in the microwave, but it didn't do anything. I figured it must have been too old. I never threw it out, though. I put it in a jar so the mice wouldn't eat it. Now I got up and put all of it in a pot of snow water and boiled and boiled it on the electric stove.

I kept hanging over the pot, fishing out the kernels to see if I could eat them yet without breaking my teeth and then putting them back to cook some more. My hand shook so bad I could hardly hold the spoon, and the pain in my stomach was like somebody stuck a knife in it. I ate half the corn before it got halfway soft. Then I ate the rest, with salt and watered-down ketchup from the bottom of a plastic bottle. Then I drank the water I boiled the corn in.

By then it was almost light. I sat in the chair in the living room and waited for the sun to hit the tops of the trees. It didn't ever. Too many clouds. It was going to be a long gray day.

I got up and went through every cupboard in the place all over again, hoping I'd find something I missed. All I found was a couple of packets of sweetener, and the mice had already got to them.

I had to leave.

I sat some more in the chair by the window and cried, because I didn't want to go. The place looked unbelievably better than when I came. Everything was all lined up nice on the shelves. I'd cleaned every part of it, including the other bedroom. On the days that the sun came out, I'd hung the moldy blankets and pillows outside over branches, and they smelled better. I washed some of the dirt off the chicken wallpaper in the kitchen, but I had to stop when the chickens started wash off too.

I always knew I'd have to go sometime. Sometime was now. I wished it wasn't, but if I didn't get going soon, I might be too weak to walk anywhere.

I heated up more water and took another bath in the dishpan and washed my hair one last time. I stripped the bed and folded the sleeping bag up neat. I left twenty dollars on the table, which I thought was plenty to cover what I used. Maybe not the firewood, but I figured I earned that. I stuck a couple of Band-Aids on my healed-up blisters and put on a thin pair of socks under my thicker ones and then my shoes.

I pulled on my pack and went out the door. Even then I kept hold of the knob for a while.

Finally I let go and looked around at everything.

Goodbye cabin. Goodbye woods. Goodbye lake.

Goodbye old moose head on the tree.

That first night that old moose seemed so creepy, and now he was just like some quiet old guy hanging around.

I was going to miss him.

I was going to miss it all.

I started walking and only looked back when I got to the turn. My mossy-roofed Hansel and Gretel house was still peeking out of the woods with my one set of tracks leading away from it. Then I couldn't see it anymore.

Most of the snow was melted again except in the woods, but I could see that nobody had been driving on this road or walking. The only tracks I saw were from deer and animals like squirrels. A robin flew across in front of me and that surprised me, because I forgot that it was spring.

It seemed like spring again now, not so cold, just kind of gloomy and misty. When I passed the log cabin on the corner, the nice one I thought of as mine all that time, I stuck out my tongue at it. Now that place with all its cushions and couches and fireplaces just seemed selfish and conceited.

"I like the other place a lot better than you," I told it. "It let me in and you didn't."

My ankle was pretty well back to normal, although I was a bit worried it would get sore again walking. It was scary to think about what kind of shape I was in when I got here that night. I could have frozen to death. It seemed almost like it happened to another person, like it was a really long time ago. I felt like I was a lot older now. And stronger and smarter, because I looked after myself for ten whole days with no help from anybody.

Only I wished I had the faintest idea what I was going to do next. You'd have thought with all that time I would have worked something out, but I didn't. The only reason I was leaving now was the food ran out. I'd have to figure what to do once I got wherever I was going.

One thing for sure, I wasn't going home. Not just because of Eddie, but all the other things. Dad really beat me bad the other time I ran away, and I wasn't away even for a whole day. What would he do for me being gone ten days? That other time he went nuts because I brought the police sniffing around. He and Mom hated it when cops or the CAS or like that showed up.

I wondered if the CAS went around to check on Nico. I wondered if the police were looking for me now.

I was quite a ways out to the highway when it started to rain. A car came up behind and I moved off to one side. It pulled up even and when I looked in the window, my heart dropped.

It was that same lady who wanted to give me a ride on the way in!

She rolled down the car window. "Where you going?"

"To town."

"Hop in. It's going to come down harder."

This time I got in. I didn't get any kind of bad feeling off her. I wasn't looking forward to walking all the way back, now I knew how far it was. Especially in the rain.

Up close she looked older than Mrs. Owen or Mom, but not that old. She had gray hair, straight and cut sort of cool, not old-ladyish. Blue eyes and glasses.

"My name's Leora," she said. "Didn't I see you walking in a week back or so? You been here all this time?"

"Yes." I told her I was staying with my sister. "Helping her with her new baby. But I have to go back to school now."

"You're gonna be late, then. It's nearly nine."

"I know. But my sister gave me a note for the office. Her car broke down."

"Which place is hers?"

She was very nosy. I sort of waved my hand behind me. I said my sister and her boyfriend only got their place last year. She wanted to know who had it before them and I said I didn't know. She asked me my name and I said Alice. She asked me questions about my family, and I made up that Mrs. Owen was my stepmother, and me and Charmaine were Mr. Owen's kids from when he was married before. I left out Anton and Nico. Too much information.

She started going on about the big snowstorm we had and being stranded before the snowplows came in.

"My hubby drives a truck and he couldn't get out to work for a whole day. How about your sister and her boyfriend?"

I said yeah, right, but I wasn't concentrating very well on what she was saying, because she had a big mug of coffee and the smell was doing my head in. All I had before I left was that popcorn and hot water.

Also she had a big fat muffin in a paper towel in the other cup holder. It looked like it had raisins in it, or maybe chocolate chips. I had to sit on my hands to keep from grabbing it.

She saw where I was looking. "Skipped breakfast, did you? Help yourself to half."

I divided it up. It was blueberries, not raisins. I tried not to stuff my half down. She just laughed. "Okay, break me off a piece and you have the rest. I don't need the calories."

It felt pretty good to be in that car, the heater going, food in my stomach after so long. The windshield wipers going back and forth was almost putting me to sleep. Maybe I did fall asleep. It didn't seem any time before we were coming into town.

"You look all done in," she said. "I can take you home. Where do you live?"

"No." I was suddenly terrified. "I have to get to school."

So she took me to school. Since it was way past nine by now, nobody was around.

I was opening the car door when Leora grabbed my arm.

"Alice, hold on a sec." I tried to pull away from her but she had a good grip. "You're a real nice kid. You wouldn't run away unless you had good reason. But think of your poor parents. They must be out of their minds worrying by now. I should take you right to the police."

I got one foot out the door. "I was at my sister's."

"Yeah, right. You're not going to level with me, are you?"

"I have to go to school. I'm late already."

"Okay, okay, don't freak out. Sit back down for a sec." When I did, she reached into her purse. "I'm gonna pretend I believe you and let the school worry about it. But here, take this." She pushed a twenty-dollar bill into my hand.

I pushed it back. "Thanks, but I don't need it." I still had thirty dollars of my money left.

"Take it, please. I'll feel better. Get yourself a sandwich."

So I took it and said thanks very much and thanks for the ride. I never expected her to be so kind, even if she was nosy.

I could feel her watching me while I walked up to the main door of the school. The grade one windows had little kids' pictures stuck up all over them and somebody's lost mitt was floating in a puddle. I wasn't thinking I'd actually go in. It was only somewhere to tell her to take me. I figured once I got out of the car I'd decide what to do next.

But I had to go right in because she was still parked, not moving away.

At least nobody was in the hall, because I was late, so I just walked out of sight of the door and stopped. I waited a bit, and after I saw she'd drove away, I went back outside.

A couple of grade-eight kids were smoking on the sidewalk across the street, but they didn't pay any attention to me. I cut through the school parking lot to the corner store and used the twenty dollars Leora gave me to buy a tuna sandwich and milk. I was still really hungry but I didn't eat it all because I thought I might get sick. I didn't have any idea what I was going to do or where I was going to go. But now I'd been to the school, it seemed normal and safe. I knew it wasn't really safe, because as soon as the teachers saw me, they'd want to know where I'd been. They'd call my parents. And probably the police.

Only I didn't have any other ideas. Maybe if it had been a nice sunny day I would have had more imagination, but it was cold and wet and windy. I told myself that if the police came to the school to take me home to my parents, I'd get away somehow. I'd pretend to be happy to go with them and as soon as I got a chance I'd just run. I didn't care if they shot me. At least it'd be better than going home.

I went back in the main school doors again. You're supposed to go to the office if you're late or you've been away, but I'd be in big trouble if I did that. I didn't even have a note. I went to the washroom to write one, but while I was washing my hands a couple of girls came in. I went into a toilet to think of what to write, and one of the girls knocked on the door and said, "You okay in there?" So I had to say yes and come out.

I headed for the stairs to go to the other girls' washroom on the second floor. I walked like I had permission so I wouldn't get asked why I was in the hall.

I got my note written this time. *Sorry Jewel has been away for 10 days but her grandmother died and she was helping her sister with her baby in Montreal. The funeral was yesterday.* Signed *Suzanne Morante.*

My gran lived in Quebec City, not Montreal, but that didn't matter. That time we visited her, Gran was old then, and she might be dead by now anyway.

When I came out of the washroom, first period was almost over, but I got a surprise when I was sneaking past the room that was my class. The door was open but nobody was inside.

I was standing there looking stupid when the art teacher, Ms. Waldie, came along.

"You look worried," she said.

"I don't know where my class is," I told her. "I only got to school now. I had to go to the dentist."

Ms. Waldie is young and nice and doesn't worry much about rules.

"There's an assembly on." She looked sort of guilty. "I should be at it too. Come on, we'll both go."

I followed her to the auditorium and we sat at the back. The principal was showing a video about Syrian refugees and how our school could help. There was pictures of kids, little babies even, living in tents because their homes were all bombed. I tried to pay attention, but I couldn't concentrate, thinking any second some teacher who wasn't like Ms. Waldie would come over and start yelling at me.

The bell went for recess and I went to my locker with everybody else. It felt weird. All I had in it was my gym shorts and T-shirt and some books and old paper. I ate some more sandwich and put my pack in and got out some stuff for class. Then I went to the office to hand in my note. I didn't have to give it to the secretary, just a grade-eight girl. She stamped it and put it in the basket and gave me a permission slip. I didn't have to talk to her or anything.

When I walked in my class, some kids turned around and looked at me, but nobody said anything. I sat in my regular seat and kept my head down.

Except then Mr. Bronson said, "Oh, Jewel, you're finally back. Did you check in at the office?" And I said yes and gave him my permission slip and he put it on the clipboard. That was all. He didn't ask me anything else.

At lunch I got the soup in the cafeteria: chili tomato. It tasted a million times better than ramen. Some girls I know,

Maya Geller and her friend Lily Larsen, came up to me and asked if I'd been sick. I said no.

"I had to go to my sister's. She had a baby and she needed some help."

"Is she doing okay?" Maya asked. Maya is the one I know best.

I couldn't help it. My eyes started filling up. All I could do was nod.

"Is the baby doing okay?" she asked me.

I said, "Yes, he's good," so they'd go away, and they finally did.

All day I kept expecting something to happen, like the secretary or vice-principal coming in and hauling me out of class. Nothing happened, though. My parents must not have told anybody I ran away. Nobody but them and me knew. So, really, nobody knew I was gone.

When three o'clock came, I didn't know what to do next. I didn't know where I was going to go. I was trying to decide if I should text Mrs. Owen and tell her I was back. If she said yes, it would be somewhere to go for a while. I went down the block from all the buses and parents picking up kids and got out my cell and turned it on. There was a bunch of texts from Mrs. Owen — one from this morning.

hope u r back could really use u tomorrow aft.

I stared at it. Then I texted, *ill come after school.*

It was still sort of raining and nasty, so I walked around the block and then went back in the school and upstairs to the resource room and did my homework. A couple of grade-eight kids were playing computer games at another table, and a boy named Jerome who is friends with Maya was reading a book. He didn't look at me. I checked on the shelves to see if they had another book by the lady that wrote that one about the girl who went to Australia. Dorothy Eden was her name. There wasn't any by her, so I got some other books.

Then everybody had to leave because the librarian was closing up. I could hear basketball practice going on in the gym, so I went and watched it. After that was over, I went back up to the second-floor washroom and peed and washed my hands and face. I was getting desperate for an idea of where to go. Maybe I should buy food and go back to the cabin. But it was so far, and it would be dark way before I got there.

I was walking back to the stairs, dragging my feet slow as I could, and I passed the art room and saw Ms. Waldie's keys were in the lock. She had a big bunch of keys.

I knocked on the door and called, "Hello?" Nobody answered. I opened the door and stuck my head in.

Nobody was in the room. Nobody was in the hall either.

What I did next I did without even thinking. I took the keys out of the lock and went inside and shut the door.

I was still just standing there, breathing hard, when I heard voices coming up the stairs. I tiptoed fast as I could go to the supplies room and went in and closed that door too. I knew from art class about the supplies room. Ms. Waldie sent us in there all the time to cut pieces off the rolls of paper on the bottom shelf. We used them for drawing. I dived over the rolls, my pack and all, and rolled to the back of the shelf. There was just enough space there to lie with my legs stretched out.

I could hear somebody unlocking the art room and opening it. Ms. Waldie's voice and some man's — Ken the custodian, it sounded like. In a little while the door to the supplies room opened and the light clicked on.

Ms. Waldie said, "I knew they wouldn't be here, Ken. I don't know what I did with them." She sounded really mad at herself.

I held my breath and stayed absolutely still. What if I sneezed? But the light went off again and they went out and shut the supplies room door. I could hear them still talking out in the art room, and while I was waiting for them to leave, I fell asleep.

Can you believe that? One minute I'm right out of my mind thinking I'm going to be caught, and the next minute I'm asleep!

When I woke up, it was pitch black. I had no idea where I was. I knew I wasn't back at the cabin — too warm, and it didn't smell right. Also, I sure wasn't in any bed. I was stiff as a board from sleeping on the hard shelf.

Then I remembered where I was and how I got there.

No light showed under the door, and even when I held my breath I couldn't hear any sound. I felt in my coat pocket for Ms. Waldie's keys. Still there. I crawled over the paper rolls and crept to the door and pulled it open the tiniest bit. Silence. I opened it further and crept out into the art room. The street lights coming through the window were bright enough so I could read my watch. Nearly ten o'clock.

The hall was lit but dim. I was terrified that any second an alarm would go off — like they might have cameras — but I had to go the washroom so bad I didn't have any choice. If the alarm went off, I'd just have to run out of the school.

I took a step. No alarm. Another step. I got all the way to the washroom with nothing happening. I didn't turn any lights on, just shuffled around and peed and washed my hands and face in the sink.

When I was walking back to the art room, all of a sudden I remembered that Ms. Waldie kept cookies in her desk drawer. Chocolate chip. I didn't think she'd miss two.

And that was the start of me living in the school.

3
The Rescuers

Maya

If it wasn't for strawberries, I might never have known about Jewel. It's like that thing about the tree falling in the forest: if a tree falls and nobody hears it, does it make a sound? Jewel was falling and nobody was listening.

So the last Friday PA day of the year I'm at the pick-your-own strawberries place with Lily and her sister Tess and their mom. Jerome isn't there because he doesn't like the outdoors.

Strawberry-picking sounds lovely and romantic but it is actually very boring and hot. I eat berries until I feel like throwing up.

Lily holds up her hands to show me how the juice makes her hands look like they're dripping blood. She says she's sweltering, and her sister Tess says, "Duh. You're wearing tights and mitts."

Lily's outfit for picking berries is fingerless gloves, ripped tights, white eyelet skirt, big sunglasses and a dollar-store seahorse tattoo on one shoulder. I've got on my camo shorts, yellow tank top, ball cap and sunblock.

"Can't we quit? We've already got a ton of berries," she says. "Like who in our family eats jam anyway?"

"Dad does," says Mrs. Larsen. "And Maya's taking some home with her. We'll pick for another ten minutes and call it quits."

Half an hour later we all go back to Lily's place and Lily and I swim in their pool and watch two movies. It's after seven o'clock by the time we get started on the jam making, but that's okay because I'm staying over. Except at ten we run out of Certo and we still have a mountain of berries to boil up.

Tess drives us to the all-night supermarket for more Certo. Tess is eighteen and she thinks she's a lot smarter and cooler than we are, but she'll drive us anywhere, anytime. She just passed her G1, so she can drive until midnight with two passengers under nineteen.

We're nearly at the Metro beside all the Subways and Burger Kings and student bars when I see this girl. She's walking along the sidewalk like she's trying to be invisible, and she's wearing shield-of-invisibility clothes.

"Hey, there's Jewel!" I say to Lily.

"What's she doing out by herself so late?" asks Tess. "And at the Hub!" The Hub is what people call the student bar area and it can get wild. I mean, Metro has security guards in its parking lot for a reason. "Is she a friend?"

"She was my lab partner last year. Stop, okay, Tess? I want to talk to her for a minute."

Tess pulls over and I jump out and run down the block, yelling, "Jewel!"

She turns. And it's her, like I thought. She looks terrified.

I smile and give a friendly little wave. "Hi, Jewel. It's me, Maya."

And she takes off — fast. But I'm faster. I'm on the track team. I catch her by the hood before the end of the block.

"Jeez, Jewel, what are you running away for? I was just saying hello."

She stares at me, breathing hard.

Tess has followed us in the van and Lily jumps out and comes over.

"What's going on, guys? What are you doing out so late, Jewel?"

Jewel starts saying something about getting milk for her mom, but Lily cuts her off. "I know you're not living with your mom. You're living at the school."

Jewel's saucer eyes get bigger. "You know?"

"I'm right, aren't I?" says Lily. "So why are you downtown this late? Shouldn't you be washing your hair in the girls' washroom? Or like cooking something over a Bunsen burner in the science room?"

Jewel's shoulders sag. "I got locked out," she says in a small voice.

"Are you going home now?" I ask her.

"Yeah."

She's not. I can tell.

Tess honks from the other side of the street.

"Hold *on*," Lily yells. And says to Jewel, "So you can't get in the school? Then where are you going?"

Tess shouts from the van, "You guys? If your friend needs a drive, I can take her."

"It's okay," Jewel says to us again. "I'll go home."

She starts walking. I grab her hood again. "You're not really going home, are you, Jewel? You're still running away."

A couple of students walk past and one guy says, "Cool it, little girls. Way past your bedtime, isn't it?"

I don't know why I don't leave Jewel alone, just let her go. I hardly know her. But I get a strong feeling that whatever's going on with her, it's not good. Seems like she's in trouble.

"You got your cell?" I ask her. I know she has one, about a hundred years old, because it fell out of her pack once in science. "Give me the number."

She stops trying to get free and says it.

I say it back. "Promise me that's the right number? Promise you'll pick up when I call?"

She nods.

"I don't believe you. Look me in the eye and swear."

"I *swear.*"

"You better not be lying to us," Lily says. "That's my sister in the van. She'll tell my parents and they'll call the police."

"We'll be calling you in ten, Jewel," I say. "You better answer your phone."

It comes out tough and mean. Her face makes me ashamed.

"We just want to help you, Jewel," I say.

We watch her hurry down the street away from us. "Remember you promised you'd answer," I call after her. "You swore."

"See?" Lily says. "She *is* living in the school, like I told you."

"Only she's locked out."

"What was all that about?" Tess asks as we get back in the van. "Were you bullying that girl?"

86

"No!" I protest. "We were trying to get her to come with us. To give her a ride. She says her parents sent her to buy milk."

Tess goes all indignant. "After ten o'clock? How old is she, anyway?"

Once we've bought the Certo and got back to the house, we run up to Lily's room so I can call Jewel.

"Can she stay in the Doll Salon?" I ask Lily. The Doll Salon is what we call the bunkie in Lily's backyard. "Just for tonight. It's an emergency."

Lily frowns. "Uhh …" She's not nuts about the idea.

"You got a better idea where she should go?"

"What are Mom and Dad going to say?"

"Duh, they won't know."

"What about Jerome? He's coming over tomorrow."

"Lily, it's not forever, just tonight. She's not going to *live* there. You saw she's totally terrified. She has no place to go. She could get attacked or raped or murdered, and if she does, it'll be your fault."

"Oh, all *right*," Lily says. "But the door's locked. I'll have to go and open it."

"Jewel might not even come," I say. "I'll text her first. Then you can call her and tell her how to get here. And be nice, okay?"

I text Jewel. *r u there?* And wait.

Is she going answer? I know I came across like a bully on the street, like Tess said.

"Has she answered yet?" Lily asks.

"Not yet."

And then I get a text back. *Yes.*

we'v got a place u cn stay so w8. Lilys calling u.

Lily calls Jewel and tells her how to get here and how to come in the back way. Jewel says she's coming. Lily tells her not to turn on any lights and she has to leave before seven tomorrow morning.

We need to go out and unlock the door and pull down the blinds. Mrs. Larsen says, "You don't need to go out there now, girls. It's nearly eleven."

"We'll only be a *minute!*" Lily screeches.

"All right, all right. You're going to be up all night. You've still got to finish that jam."

It does only take a minute. Lily leaves Jewel a bag of chips and a banana and a flashlight.

"You didn't tell her about the dolls, did you?" I ask.

"No, but I told her there's a bathroom."

I text Jewel. *Its nice. lots of dolls. sorry about the dark.*

im not afraid of the dark, she texts back.

Seems like she's afraid of something a lot scarier than the dark.

I keep looking out the window before we go to bed but I can't see if Jewel came like she promised. Next morning, way too early, Lily shakes me awake.

"Jewel definitely stayed in the Doll Salon. She's not there now, but she was. I left those chips and the banana with the flashlight, and they're gone. I mean, the flashlight's still there, but not the food."

How Lily came to have the Doll Salon is this. Lily had a ton of Barbies, so the Christmas she turned eleven, Mr. Larsen built her an amazing doll showcase to go in her bedroom, with glass shelves and spotlights. Lily got little wire things to make the dolls stand up, and she was always rearranging them.

Then last summer Lily's dad helped her redecorate her bedroom to make it less little-girly and they decided the doll showcase didn't fit with the design scheme. Also, it took up so much space. So her dad moved it to the bunkie in the backyard. It's a very cool bunkie with its own bathroom and microwave and fridge, but nobody uses it because the Larsens' house is huge. The whole basement is finished, with a jacuzzi and a 54-inch screen.

Lily has a lot more dolls now (122 last time we counted), so her dad put up more shelves and an IKEA cupboard with drawer dividers for all their shoes and handbags and underwear and other accessories. And a workbench, with stools to sit at. The floor is black-and-white checkerboard tiles and Lily's mom made black-and-white blinds for the windows, and we got black-and-white chenille throws for the couches and the recliner. We already painted the walls Bangkok Sunset.

I moved some dolls over and then Jerome did too. About twenty are mine and fifteen are Jerome's — nine male, five female, one not sure.

The Doll Salon is our club, but it's also to make money. Lily got the idea from going to doll shows with her mom. Sometimes on Saturday mornings we go around the yard sales and Lily sees some filthy dirty-looking naked thing with matted hair and says, "Oh, look! That's a Benefit Ball Barbie. Poor sad thing! Little people aren't supposed to look like that!" And she'll get it for like fifty cents. Or "That's a First Edition Canadian Barbie!" (Mountie outfit, except the pants and boots are missing). Or it could be the first Ken doll to have bendable elbows. She'll pay like a dollar for it and a month later she'll have it fixed up and sell it online and she'll have made, say, seventy dollars. For some OOAKs — One-of-a-Kinds — she makes a lot more.

What you do is, you scrub the doll with alcohol until it's clean and shiny (if nobody or their dog has been chewing on it — we don't buy those ones). The lips might be faded or the eyebrows worn off, so Lily repaints them. Or Jerome does. If the hair is bad, Lily cuts it out and takes the head off and reroots it. We all do rerooting, but Lily is fastest.

I used to love the dolls when I was little but not as much now. I loved when we made up stories about them and they had adventures. Now it's all about how good the dolls look and how they live their lives, like celebrities. Like if they want to fly to Ibiza for a party or go on an Antarctica cruise to see penguins, they do. They get the outfit and go. If they want to be a business tycoon, they get the hair and the briefcase and the suit. If they want to be a tennis star, same thing. It's all about how they're dressed. That doesn't interest me so much.

I do like making money off them, like one Teen Talk Barbie we got, that was amazing. And having the Doll Salon is fantastic, so I don't blame Lily for not wanting to risk it. She's very definite about that.

"She can't stay in the Salon again. If Dad or Mom found out —"

"I get it, Lily. Except what's she going to do? She's locked out of the school, and she *really* doesn't want to go home."

"But why? What's so terrible about going home? Is she like abused, or what? We need her to talk to us."

I text Jewel to meet us at the Italia Tea Shop at two. I'm not sure if she will, but she texts back *ok*.

The three of us arrive at the Italia at the exact same time, Lily and me from one direction, Jewel from another. Anybody'd think we were just ordinary friends meeting up. Or not too ordinary. Lily's got on her red cowboy boots and a short red skirt and her hair is coming out the top of her head like a fountain. I'm in my jean shorts from yesterday with a tee that looks like it's covered in spider webs and spiders. Jewel is dressed the same as always — like invisible.

She says hi. She looks unhappy, jumpy. Maybe she's hungry.

"Get whatever you want," I tell her. "I'm paying."

"I've got my own money."

Mr. Brunetti is behind the counter. He's as old as my granddad, and his eyebrows look like haystacks. He calls us princesses. Well, mostly he calls Lily that.

"Mr. Brunetti, you can't say that. It's sexist and classist," Lily tells him. But he never learns.

Today he says, "Here comes the teeny-boppers." It's probably an Italian expression, from some other century.

"You want us to go to Tim Hortons instead?" I say back.

"No, no, little princesses' money is good here."

We go to the Italia because it's not crowded with university students like Starbucks or David's. Also, it has good tea. We like tea, not coffee. I like cocoa spearmint, which doesn't sound like tea but actually it is. Lily gets organic crème brûlée. Jewel asks for regular tea with milk — invisible people's tea.

We're just sitting down in our regular booth when it gets really noisy outside. A bunch of motorcycles stop at the lights and start revving their engines. Jewel scoots into the corner of the booth out of sight of the window and scrunches down. Her face is white.

Even with the street door closed, we have to shout with the engines roaring and revving.

"What's the matter?" I ask Jewel. "Don't worry, it's just old guys on bikes."

She doesn't say anything until the bikes roar off and it's quiet again. Then she blurts out, "My dad knows bikers. He said if I gave him trouble like my sister, if I ran away, he said the gang has people everywhere and they'd find me."

We stare at her. In two years I never heard her say that much.

"They're only old guys," I say again.

"With white ponytails," says Lily. "Out for a drive with their old girlfriends. Their old ladies. They wouldn't hurt you."

Jewel is really concentrating on pouring her tea. At the Tea Shop the tea bags hang on top of the pot from a little stick, and Jewel's tea slops around it on the table. She goes red and mops at it with her napkin.

"That happens to everybody," I say. "Did you sleep okay last night?"

She nods, looks up at Lily. "Thanks for letting me stay last night. I really appreciate it."

"No problem," says Lily. "So how long have you been living in the school?"

Jewel sort of jumps when Lily says that, but there's nobody close enough to hear anything.

"Promise never to tell?"

"Promise," we say.

"I been there a while," she says.

"Like quite a while?" Lily says. "Because that time I saw you drying your hair in the girls' washroom, that was May."

"Since near the start of April," says Jewel.

"April!" Lily inhales her tea. "That's like over two months! How could you live in school that long without anybody noticing?"

"I'm careful."

"Since April, your parents don't know where you are?" I ask her.

It's unbelievable. If my mother doesn't know where I am for two minutes, there's a major panic.

"Since March," she says. "I ran away in March. But I stayed in a cabin at first, not the school. A cabin in the woods."

"In the woods!" Lily yelps. "Nobody could stay in the woods in March. There was *snow*."

"I stayed in a cabin. Near the conservation area."

"Whose cabin? How did you get there?" I ask.

"I had to walk a really long way. I thought I knew a place to stay from when we went to the conservation area, but it was locked up. I couldn't get in. I found another place, though."

"How long did you stay?" Lily asks.

"I kind of lost track of time. Ten days, maybe?"

"Ten days!" How could anybody who's only thirteen stay in a cabin by themselves for ten days? That's like solitary confinement. I'd be chewing the doorknobs.

"But it was *freezing*," Lily says. "Wasn't there a huge snow-storm?"

"Yeah, and I was so stupid, I didn't figure out how to turn on the electricity. Until the very end — April Fools' Day! But there was a woodstove, so I could keep warm okay. And I could cook on it."

"I wouldn't even know how to start a woodstove," I say. "Nobody helped you?"

"No, nobody was there except me. Except on the way back, a lady gave me a ride so I didn't have to walk the whole way. She took me to school and waited, so I had to go in."

I remember that day. I remember how upset she looked. And she smelled like woodsmoke.

"You told us then you were at your sister's," Lily says. "You said she was having a baby. So that was a lie."

Jewel just nods. She's not ashamed of getting caught lying.

"What I don't get," I say, "is why there was never anything like on TV or anything, about you being missing."

Jewel fiddles with her tea bag on its little stick. "My parents didn't tell the police."

"Your parents didn't tell the *police*?" Lily shrieks.

"Shut up, Lily," I say. Mr. Brunetti is looking over and wagging his finger at us.

"Okay, sorry, but that's just totally weird. Like they still don't know where you are and they still haven't told the police? "

Jewel shrugs and stirs her tea really carefully, like making sure it has no lumps.

"What did the vice-principal say when you came back?" I ask.

"Nothing. Nobody said anything. I thought for sure they would. I just came back and handed in my note and sat in my seat like usual and nobody said anything."

"Not even the teacher? Didn't Mr. Bronson say *anything*?"

"I had a note from my mother."

"What do you mean, a note from your mother?" I ask. "She doesn't even know you're back, you said."

Jewel smiles a little. "I write my notes."

"How could you hide in the *school*?" Lily asks. "Where do you *sleep*? On the couches in the staff room?"

Jewel shakes her head. "No, because some teachers stay at school late sometimes. Or some of them come in really early."

"In the gym, on the mats?" I ask.

"No."

"Well, where?"

"You won't tell?"

We promise.

"In the art room. I got Ms. Waldie's keys."

"Aack! The *art room*?" Lily cries. "The floor is totally filthy!"

"I don't sleep on the floor. I sleep in the supplies cupboard. On the bottom shelf, at the back."

Lily shudders. "The supplies cupboard. How creepy is that?"

"It's not so bad," Jewel says. "I got a yoga mat, and a floaty mattress from the dollar store. I keep them in my locker. And I got an LED flashlight so I can read. I leave the door to the art room open a crack, so I can see light from the streetlights. And I got a little alarm clock. I set it for five, before anybody comes in. It's already light then."

A floaty mattress and a little alarm clock. She makes it sound cozy.

"But how do you like keep clean?"

96

"I know," Lily says. "The washroom. You wash your hair there."

"I used to. Not after you saw me."

But her hair doesn't look dirty.

"Where I babysit, I can take showers if I do it fast, when the people are out at the store. The boys don't notice, I let them watch TV. And I can wash my clothes when I'm there. I can eat there too, when I feed the boys. I'm allowed to. Plus I can buy food with my babysitting money. I only have to sleep in the school."

It's weird how she says it so matter of fact. Like it's normal. It's not normal.

Her parents live in the same city as her and they don't know where she is? It's not like she's in some movie. She's a *kid*.

"Only they changed the locks now," she says sadly. "My key to the front door doesn't work anymore."

The big question is, why doesn't she go home?

When I ask it, she frowns and looks down at the table.

"Did your dad hit you? Because he's not allowed to do that, you know."

"It's not safe at home," she says finally. She mumbles something about some drunk guy coming into her room.

"But it's your *home*!" I say. "You should have told your parents what happened!"

She gives me an angry look. "They knew. Dad saw, Dad hit him. It didn't make any difference. It didn't with my sister either."

"Then you should tell Mr. Puddicombe." That's the school counselor. "He'll tell the police."

97

"No!" she cries. "The police'll only make it worse. They'll make me go home. I'm not going home." Her voice goes up and she pushes her tea away. She tries to get out of the booth. "I have to get going."

Only she can't, because we've got her blocked in.

"You can't go yet," I say.

Her eyes go wide and scared, like I'm bullying her. I hold up my hands.

"Whoa! I just mean we need to know more if we're going to help you. We need to understand what's going on. We won't try to make you do anything, Jewel. We only want to help."

"You can't help," she says flatly. "No one can."

"We can," I say. "We're your friends."

She shakes her head. Meaning, we're not her friends. Like we know her but we're not friends with her. But we do want to help. I do, anyway.

"We can find a way to help, can't we?" I say to Lily.

Lily nods. "Yeah."

"You promised you wouldn't tell," Jewel says. "Not anybody. Not anything."

"We won't tell," I say. "You can totally trust us. We already thought you were living in the school and we didn't tell anybody, right?" I don't say that we changed our mind about it because Lily and Jerome followed her and they thought she was living in foster care. I guess she just went to the place she babysits. Jerome might have forgotten all that by now. And anyway, it's just Jerome and nobody believes half the things he says.

98

I can see Jewel still wants to leave, but she's calmed down a bit. There's lots more I want to find out about that doesn't add up. Like for a start, babysitting.

"Aren't you kind of young to be a sitter? Aren't you thirteen, same as us?"

"It used to be my sister Charmaine's job. I was twelve when she left, but Mrs. Owen asked me if I could help out until she got somebody else. Only she never did. They don't pay me a lot, but now I don't have to give any of it to Mom."

"Your mom takes your babysitting money?" Lily looks indignant. Our mothers don't take our doll money. Like they wouldn't do that. That wouldn't happen.

"Not all of it," Jewel says. "I didn't give her all of it. I kept some. Now I keep it all."

"Do the Owens know you're living in the school?" I ask. "Do they know you're not going home?"

"They don't know I ran away, even. When I went, I left Mrs. Owen a message that my parents took me to Montreal. When I came back, I called her and she said she got somebody else to look after the boys, but the boys liked me better."

"Doesn't Mrs. Owen talk to your parents?" I persist.

"No. She just calls my phone and we arrange it. My parents don't know I got a phone."

"But don't the Owens live near you?" I ask. "Somebody in your family might see you going there. Like Anton."

"Anton wouldn't tell, though, would he?" Lily says.

"He'd tell," Jewel says. "But he doesn't ever go down the Owens' street. It's three blocks away and his high school is the other way."

"Somebody else that knows you or your family might see you," says Lily.

"Nobody notices me."

"Somebody might, if they were looking for you." I can see the wheels turning in Lily's head. "You need to be really disguised," she tells Jewel. "A complete change of image." She claps her hands. She's already excited about the idea. "First I need to cut your hair. Like make it really different from what it is now. Let's go back to the Doll Salon right now and I'll do it."

Jewel doesn't look too sure.

"I guess now you know why we call it the Doll Salon," I say.

"Didn't you *love* it?" Lily says.

"Oh, yes, it's really nice. It was just ..." Jewel looks embarrassed. "Kind of creepy. All those little faces looking at me. There's so many of them."

She's been living in the art supplies cupboard, and doll faces creep her out?

Suddenly she tenses up. She's looking at the door. Somebody just came in and is staring over at us. It's a good thing Jewel's trapped in the booth or she'd be gone.

It's a boy in an army jacket.

"Hi, guys," says Jerome. He sticks out his bottom lip. "Why are you having a party and you didn't invite *me*?"

I don't see how anybody could be afraid of Jerome. He's about as fierce as a tree.

He's older than us, fourteen, and in grade eight, but he's our friend. Because we're so smart and beautiful.

Also, he doesn't have too many other friends. He used to be friends with Billy Gretz who was the best runner in our school, but Billy moved away. Jerome didn't have a friend then so he started hanging around us. He says he likes being with us more than he likes being with guys. Guys aren't as fun as us. But mostly it's dolls. He and Lily make quite a bit of money off them, which Jerome really likes.

He drops his army surplus bag on the floor next to the booth and goes to the counter to order.

"I'm getting us *cake*," he yells over his shoulder. "Hi, Mr. Brunetti."

"We won't tell him anything you said," I whisper to Jewel. I mouth to Lily, *Don't say anything* — and point at Jewel.

"You know Jerome, right?" I say to her. "He does dolls with us."

He's on his way over with his tea and hears. "Oh, *thanks* for blowing my cover, Maya."

"Jewel won't tell," I say. As if it's about him.

"Hi, Jewel," he says, like he's never seen her before. I see him wondering what she's doing with us.

"I do ink," he tells Jewel. "*Manly* stuff. I tattoo dolls."

"We're professionals," Lily explains.

"Cake?" He shoves it toward Jewel, a huge slice of chocolate cheesecake with four forks. She shakes her head. "C'mon," he says to her, "you know you want it."

Sometimes Jerome says he's gay, and sometimes he says he's bi. He started a LGBT club at school, but only two other people joined, Brianna Davis and Emma Zarkos, and Jerome quit. Sometimes he does stuff he thinks is cool but is really not. Like he got both eyebrows pierced and once he grew a soul patch under his lip. He's the only boy in grade eight with facial hair. Another time he wanted to get his knuckles tattooed but he couldn't decide what four-letter words would be best.

"Jewel saw the Doll Salon," I tell him. "She can't believe how many dolls we have."

Jerome's eyebrows go way up. I shouldn't have said anything about it. He knows we don't usually show other people the Doll Salon. In fact we made a big deal out of showing him the first time. Mrs. Larsen says it's not generally a good idea for people to know what's out in their backyard. That many dolls are worth a lot of money. Of course they're insured and there's locks on the door and the windows, but no point drawing attention.

I can see Lily is itching to leave. She wants to get cutting Jewel's hair. We tell Jerome we have to go and he says great, he'll come with us. Lily tells him he can't because it's a private thing.

"Heartless bitches." He grabs what's left of the cake and

eats it himself. Then he pulls his messenger bag over his head and takes off.

Jewel watches him. "He's mad. It's my fault. He doesn't like me."

"Don't worry. It's not you. He's just a drama queen," says Lily. "I'll text him later and he'll be completely over it."

Jerome is our friend, but that doesn't mean we have to have him around all the time. He talks too loud and he can get hysterical, so he isn't too good at keeping secrets.

He doesn't need to know anything about Jewel.

When we get to Lily's, she goes in the house to get her hair-cutting scissors and her style magazines. I take Jewel in the backyard to the Doll Salon. She's not exactly happy with Lily's plan but so far she's going along with it.

Lily comes back and sits Jewel on a stool at the work-bench with the magazines. "Look through them and find a picture of somebody with hair that you like."

Lily can do anything with hair — people's or dolls'. She can do any kind of braids you can think of. French fishtail, four-strand, upside-down. She does her own hair herself. Sometimes she'll have three or four hairstyles in one day, like an updo and a messy bun and ringlets and braids.

Jewel picks out a style that looks practically the same as what she already has.

"Nope," says Lily. "It's supposed to be a disguise, remember? It has to be totally different." She picks up the scissors. "Trust me." She chops.

Jewel looks down at the big piece of hair on the floor and goes green.

"Whoops!" Lily squeals. She sees Jewel's face. "Just kidding. I meant to do that."

"It'll grow back," I say to Jewel. "I mean, if you don't love it. But you'll love it. Lily does really good haircuts, and it'll be way cooler looking."

Jewel starts to get off the stool. "I don't want to be cooler. I don't want people looking at me."

Lily pushes her back down and pats her on the shoulder.

"Trust me," she says again. "Maya means you'll fit in better. This is so the right thing to do. Really."

Soon there's lots more hair on the floor. Jewel's head looks pretty weird until Lily leads her into the bathroom and shampoos her in the sink. Then she works in some product and blow-dries and scrunches. I watch.

Finally she stands back.

"So. What do we think?" She hands Jewel a mirror.

Jewel frowns at herself. Lily shows her how she can see the back of her head in the doll showcase mirror.

"It's really nice, Jewel," I tell her.

Actually, it's amazing. Lily made the back short but left it longer on the sides and wavy. It looks more up to date. "You don't have to worry about standing out. You look like a lot of other girls. Like Lexa Buckingham." Who is a very cool girl in grade eight. "And way different from what you did. It's a good disguise."

"It'll be even better if we change the color," says Lily.

"It's okay like it is," Jewel says quickly. She probably doesn't want to end up with purple hair. She's still looking at herself in the mirror and turning her head back and forth. I see her smile the tiniest smile at her reflection. She can see she looks good.

"Now," Lily says briskly, "she needs new outfits. She can't go on wearing the same thing all the time."

"It's so she doesn't get noticed," I say. "So nobody sees her. It works."

"No, it doesn't," says Lily. "I noticed how bad she dressed."

"Okay, but you would."

"Stop talking about me like I'm not here," Jewel says.

Actually, that's not how we're talking about her. We're talking about her like she's a doll. I can see she doesn't like the idea of us dressing her. I mean, Lily is really pretty and has hair like black silk and walks like a model, but the main reason people pay attention to her is because of how she dresses. Like today, the red cowboy boots and the red mini.

Jewel looks over at me. "I'd wear what Maya wears."

"That's because Maya dresses boring," says Lily. "Almost as bad as you." She puts a finger against her lips for a minute. "We could have a clothes swap."

Brilliant idea. That way Jewel can pick out what she wants and not end up wearing striped tights and red suspenders.

"I don't have anything to swap," she says.

"That's okay. We don't need invisible clothes," says Lily.

Lily is totally pleased with herself for the way Jewel's hair turned out and the idea of dressing her in outfits. Only Jewel's appearance is not the main problem and it never was. The main problem is where she's going to stay now that she can't get in the school anymore.

"But it's only the weekends that I can't get in," she says when I say that.

I ask her how that works.

"Well, if it's Monday, I can still get in the school after I babysit because they don't lock up until later. There's sports and music and drama rehearsals. Other school nights are the same, even Friday. They leave the doors open until nine, and I get back from babysitting before eight. It's only locked Saturdays and Sundays, and my keys don't work anymore. I tried them on all the outside doors."

"Starting in three weeks, it'll be locked all summer," I say.

"And anyway, if it's summer, even if your keys still worked, people would notice you going in and out. There wouldn't be other kids around."

Jewel looks miserable. "I know."

"Couldn't you stay with the people you babysit for?" I ask.

She shakes her head, looking a bit startled at the way her cut hair swings. "They don't know I ran away. I told them I went to Montreal because my gran died. If they knew I ran away, they'd get in trouble if they didn't tell the police. I'm worried they'll find out. They always want to drive me home at nights, but I don't let them."

"Why can't she stay here in the Doll Salon?" I ask Lily. "I mean, until we figure something out? It's your private space. Nobody in your family comes in without asking. They won't know if Jewel is here."

Lily doesn't look happy that I brought the idea up again.

"My parents could come in. It's their property." She's got a bald doll head on her lap on her little cushion, rerooting it with long silver hair. Its blue eyes stare at us. "In the summertime they sit out on the deck. They would notice somebody was there."

We'd all be in trouble then, especially Jewel.

Jewel is gazing around at all the dolls.

"How many of those are there?" she asks.

"Two hundred?" Lily shrugs. "I didn't count lately. They're not all mine. Some are Maya's or Jerome's, and some are Mom's. She used to collect Barbies, but she let me have all her dolls since she got to be a lawyer. I sold a lot of them. I mean, I asked her first. I'm not so much into Barbies now. There's more money in Fashion Royalty dolls."

Jewel's eyes widen. "A lot of money?"

Lily nods. "Yeah, even from Barbies if they're vintage or collectables. Like a Teen Talk Barbie that Maya got at a church sale, we got three hundred for it. And Jerome makes a lot from tattoos."

Jewel points at the little bald head on the cushion on Lily's lap. "Why are you doing that?"

"Rerooting? It's a special order. I can get nearly a hundred dollars for it."

"But how do you know about all that?"

"The Internet, doll boards, places like that."

"Okay," I say, getting us back to the point. "The Doll Salon could still be one place for Jewel to stay, Lily. Like if it's raining, your parents won't be outside." I have another idea. "She can come to our houses for sleepovers."

We have sleepovers all the time. Jerome comes too, but he goes home after the last movie.

"So on Saturday nights we can have a sleepover at your house or my house, and on Sunday afternoons we can have a meeting out here and lock up and leave, only Jewel can stay."

Lily frowns down at the bald doll head. "Well, okay, maybe. Only, what's she going to do all week when it's summer?"

"I don't know. Let's have a sleepover at my house tonight and we can make a plan."

I call Mom to ask if it's okay but I know it won't be a problem. She and Dad aren't going out or anything.

"Lily's coming but not Jerome. We have a new friend we want to invite."

"Oh? Who's that?" Mom sounds surprised. We don't usually ask anybody new.

"Um … Anna? She's in our class." Actually, there's two Annas in our class. Jewel isn't one of them.

Except that two minutes later my mom calls back and says, "Maya, I don't know Anna's parents. I'd better call them and introduce myself. They won't want her staying overnight with people they don't know."

I think fast. "I'll, um, get the number and call you back with it, Mom."

"You don't have it in your phone?"

"I need to find it."

I hang up. "Sorry about the Anna, Jewel," I say. "I had to think fast."

"I don't mind," she says. "I like Anna for a name."

"My mom wants to talk to your parents to make sure it's okay with them for you to come over."

"No!" She shoots off the stool and starts for the door.

"Calm down. I *know* that," I say. "I need to figure out what to do."

Then Lily says, "I know. I'll call your mom, Maya, and pretend I'm Jewel's mother. Anna's mom."

"How's that gonna work? My mom will see it's you from the call display."

"Okay, I'll use Jewel's." Lily puts out her hand to Jewel.

"Won't my mother know you're not Jewel's mother?" I say.

"No, daahling," Lily drawls. Lily gets the main parts in all the school plays because she's fantastic at voices. She can do almost anybody, Oprah, whatever. Sometimes she'll call me using her mom's voice and I won't even clue in. Well, for half a minute anyway.

Jewel hands over her clunky phone and Lily starts punching in my home number. Then she stops. "Jewel, does your mother have the same last name as you?"

"Yeah, Morante."

"And what's her first name?"

I say, "On the call display it says C. Morante."

"But that's not my mother," Jewel says. "That's my sister, Charmaine. It's her phone."

"Your mother can be named … Celeste. No, Christina," Lily decides. She dials the landline at my house and waits until my mom picks up.

"Hello, Mrs. Geller?" she says in her deepest voice. "This is Chrrristina Morante." She's laying it on very thick in this throaty voice like Jewel's mother is some Russian spy. "Anna has called me to say your daughter has kindly invited her to a sleepover at your home tonight."

She listens for a bit and then says, "My daughter Anna talks about your daughter Maya all the time … No, that

110

won't be necessary. She's at her friend Lily Larsen's house now, and they can all walk over together ... A toothbrush? So verrry kind of you. Thank you so *verrry* much."

Lily ends the call and bows. "Applause, please!"

Jewel looks at her in awe. "I couldn't ever do that. A voice like that, I mean."

"I'm good," Lily says. "Not to be too modest."

And then my cell goes. Uh-oh, it's Mom.

"Everything's arranged," she tells me. "Anna's mother just called. Tell Anna she's very welcome, will you? Oh, dear, I forgot to ask her mother if she'll be picking Anna up tomorrow morning. I'd better call her back."

"Don't bother, Mom," I say. "Lily's sister can drive Anna home."

"So what's your message on your cell?" Lily asks Jewel when I hang up. "Maybe we should change it. In case our parents call it. I can do your mother's voice for it. *You've reached Chrrristin-aa ...*"

"No!" Jewel hugs her phone like it's a kitten Lily wants to take away from her and drown. "It's my sister's message. Charmaine's voice."

"But if our parents call it, it needs to sound like it's your mother's phone," Lily says.

Jewel shakes her head harder. "It's the message Mrs. Owen hears if she calls about babysitting and leaves a message. She'd wonder if it got changed to somebody else's voice. Somebody else she doesn't even know."

"Only —" Lily starts.

"No," Jewel says again. "It's all I've got left. Of Charmaine."

Which is creepy.

I put my phone on speaker and punch in Jewel's number. When her phone starts ringing, she gives a surprised little squawk.

"Don't answer," I tell her. "I want to hear her."

And then a voice sort of like Jewel's but older says, *"You've reached —"* and gives the phone number. No name, just the number. And says to leave a message.

"She sounds nice," I say.

"She is," says Jewel.

"She doesn't sound too much like a kid," Lily says. "Young, but she could still be a grown-up."

Lily goes into her house to tell her mom about the sleepover and then the three of us walk over to my place. It's clouded over now and I hear thunder rumbling. We're a block away when big fat drops start plopping down. That great rain smell comes up from the sidewalk, and then it starts really pouring. We run the rest of the way and get in the door half-soaked. We're all laughing and Mom comes out with a towel and dries us down — Jewel too. She looks a bit surprised.

It rains all the rest of the day so we stay downstairs in the family room, lying on the couches watching movies with Beezer the Shih Tzu (really, that's actually what they call that kind of little dog), the two Mexicats, Salsa and Taco, and Claire's gerbil. Since Claire is there too, we have to remember to call Jewel "Anna" in front of her. Mom makes us pasta and apple crisp from the freezer.

I flip on the gas fireplace with the remote to make it cozier. Jewel blinks at it.

"It's so real. With the little logs."

"Does it remind you of when you were at that cabin?" I whisper to her, so Claire doesn't hear.

"The one there didn't have any remote," she whispers back. She almost made a joke.

Lily calls her sister Tess to drop off her pajamas and toothbrush, which she forgot, and also get her a package of L'Oréal Féria Plum hair color and a couple of frozen four-cheese pizzas from Shoppers. Lily is still putting pressure on Jewel to color her hair. But Jewel won't budge, so Lily decides to do her own. We heat the pizza in the downstairs microwave while Lily streaks her hair. It comes out more auburn than plum, so it wouldn't have done that much for disguising Jewel. Then we eat the pizza, blow up the air mattresses, make Claire go upstairs to bed, and get into our pajamas. I lend Jewel some of mine. We're almost the same size.

I've been looking forward all evening to Claire being out of the way so we can hear some more about Jewel's life. Me and Lily have to ask a lot of questions before she finally opens up a bit. She tells us more about staying in that cabin and what a disgusting smelly place it was at first. Her feet were wrecked from walking so far and she bashed her hand with a rock and all she had to eat was oatmeal and ramen.

"What's ramen?" Lily asks.

Jewel looks amazed that anybody doesn't know what ramen is.

"I also ate some stuff in cans I found in the cupboard," she goes on. "But I left money to pay for it."

"I'd be so freaked out," Lily says. "I've never been by myself for a *day*, let alone ten days or whatever. I've never been by myself for an *hour*. When I'm not asleep, I mean."

"And not in the woods," I say.

"Being by myself doesn't bother me," Jewel says. "Only I was worried the people who owned it would come back."

"I still don't get why you had to run away in the first place," Lily says. "Your dad threw out that sleazy guy that was bothering you, right? And I don't get why you can't go home. Because they'd be really mad at you? Wouldn't they be happy you're back and not still lost?"

Jewel goes stone-faced. "I don't want to talk about it. I'm really tired." She does look totally exhausted. Her face has gone gray and flat. It's late for her for to be up, I guess. Especially seeing she's used to sleeping in the supplies cupboard and getting up at five in the morning.

We turn out the lights but we still talk some more. Or Lily and me do anyway. Jewel pulls the sleeping bag up around her ears and turns toward the wall, and it seems like she goes to sleep right away. But in the middle of the night I wake up, and the moon is shining in the window, and I see her lying on her back with her eyes open.

"Jewel?" I whisper, and she shuts them.

Suddenly this memory pops into my head. It might have been a year ago, and me and Lily were walking past this girl sitting by herself on the steps outside the school eating her lunch. There wasn't any reason to notice her, except that this seagull was walking back and forth watching her eat. She was trying to ignore it, and the gull kept squawking at her to give it some of her lunch. Then it got fed up and started shrieking at the top of its lungs. You could have heard it blocks away. The girl — it had to be Jewel, for sure — stamped her feet to get it to leave her alone.

Poor Jewel, trying to be invisible, and that bird was not helping things.

She's still trying to be invisible. Only, too bad, we saw her.

When I wake up, Jewel is already dressed and sitting on the couch.

"I've been reading, waiting for you to wake up." She shuts the book. "I have to get going."

I squint at the clock. "It's not even nine."

"I slept in to seven. Two hours ago."

"You can't go yet. We told Mom that Lily's sister would drive you home. And you didn't even have breakfast yet."

Besides, Mom has some big idea we're having a Sunday morning muffin bake-off. Only, Lily is still asleep, and I'm not going to be the one to wake her up.

"It can be me and Claire against you two," Mom says. She hands us the muffin book. "Choose your weapon."

Jewel-Anna looks through the book like Mom tells her to. After a while she shows me a recipe for bacon and blueberry muffins.

"You put a little piece of bacon in the bottom of the tin, just raw. It doesn't have to be cooked first."

"Good choice," Mom says. "We have bacon, and there's a bag of blueberries in the freezer." She gets out all the stuff we need and Anna-Jewel starts measuring. She does it very scientifically, like when we were lab partners.

"I see you're a cook, Anna," Mom says. Anna-Jewel looks pleased.

After we get everything stirred and poured and the muffins put in the oven, Jewel starts in cleaning up. She rinses everything before she puts it in the dishwasher.

"Are you seeing this, Maya? Claire?" Mom cries. "She cooks and then she cleans up! I love this girl."

Anna-Jewel goes all pink.

While the muffins are baking, we go back downstairs and turn the TV on loud to wake up Lily. She's the muffin judge. She gives me and Jewel the prize, but Mom and Claire's pineapple-bran ones get a good mark too.

"If you didn't put bran in them, Mom, ours would have won," Claire says. She is such a poor loser.

I can see Jewel is really itching to get going again. She doesn't want to wait around for Tess to come and pick her and Lily up.

"It's okay for me to walk home," she tells Mom. "It's not far. I'm allowed. I do it all the time."

I don't think that's going to work, but Mom just says, "Phone your mother first and tell her you're on your way."

Jewel says she will. "Thanks for everything, Mrs. Geller. I had a lovely time." She's heading out the door while Mom is still telling her to come again soon.

I run after her. Where's she going, anyway?

When I ask, she just looks at me like it's none of my business. "Just around."

"Like just around where?"

She shrugs. "The library, and like that."

I tell her I'll text her to say when to come to Lily's for supper and another sleepover.

She rubs the toe of her shoe on the sidewalk. "Does it have to be supper *and* a sleepover? Can't I just come later, like the time before, and sleep in the doll place?"

"The library closes early on weekends. Where are you going to go all that time?"

She just gives me that look again.

But then I think, maybe she's right. Maybe another sleepover won't work out. Tomorrow's a school day and Mom will think I should be doing homework, even though it's June and no teachers give us any homework now. I tell Jewel I'll text her and let her know if it's okay with Lily. She heads off, and I go back in my house and ask.

"I guess so," Lily says reluctantly. "Tell her I'll put the key under the flowerpot outside. But tell her she has to be absolutely sure nobody else is around."

Mom comes downstairs to collect up the sheets and blankets. "I like your friend Anna, girls. She seems like a really nice person. Well mannered and thoughtful. And quiet." She gives Lily a nudge. "Unlike some of your friends."

Lily rolls her eyes.

When we get to school next morning, I ask Lily if it went okay with Jewel in the Doll Salon.

"I think so," she says. "I looked out the window a couple of times and couldn't see any light. I pulled the blinds down again and she uses one of those little dollar-store book lights to read." Then she goes all ice-princessy. "But, Maya, no way she can stay there in the summer. Once it starts getting hot, my parents sit out by the pool a lot at night. I told you. They'd notice if she was in the Doll Salon."

"Don't worry, we'll have something sorted out by then." I hope, at least. We haven't yet. Anyway, now it's not the weekend, Jewel can go back to living in her art-room cupboard.

We don't exactly hang out with her now — I mean, she's in the other grade seven class — but she usually eats lunch with us.

Jerome thinks that's weird. "She's not in the Doll Club, right? She doesn't seem very dolly to me. And like not to be mean, but she's *boring*."

"That is a mean thing to say, actually," I say.

"Huh," he snorts, but he looks embarrassed. He's not really mean. He's just jealous. I guess he's a bit threatened, like we're dropping him for her and he can't see why.

But we can't have him there when Jewel's around. He'd want to be in on everything. It's not a good idea to have more people knowing than absolutely necessary. Also, we promised Jewel we wouldn't tell anybody. Jerome isn't just anybody, but he isn't too careful about what he says.

He's noticed she looks different from the way she did. "Little Miss Clone," he's started calling her. Not to her face, of course. He thinks she's imitating us. He thinks she's our fan.

"I styled her hair," Lily says. "Doesn't it look totally better?"

Jerome stares over at Jewel standing in the line-up for soup. He tosses his hair out of his eyes.

"Yeah, but she should lose the homeless outfit. Lily, I gotta work on that Harley tattoo doll. I got an order for it. I'm coming over after school." All his inks are at the Doll Salon.

"Okay," she tells him. "I've got stuff to do too. I have to pack doll heads for shipping."

"Will Clonette be there?"

"No. Just me and Maya."

So that week goes pretty much the same as usual.

The next two weeks go pretty smooth too. Jewel — Anna, I have to remember — meets all our parents and they don't pick up on anything funny. On school nights she sleeps at school and doesn't get caught. I worry she will, but she's got that shield-of-invisibility thing. I guess if she can live in the school for two months before we finally noticed it — and that was even after Lily saw her washing her hair in the washroom — she can fly under the radar a bit longer.

On the third Friday, we have a sleepover at Lily's. We're going to finally have the clothes swap too, so I bring some stuff. It's a stinking hot afternoon and Lily has a great pool, so we swim before supper. Lily's sister Tess lends Jewel one of her old one-pieces. Tess already recognized Jewel from the night outside Metro, but that's okay. We must not have said Jewel's name in front of her then, or if we did, Tess doesn't remember.

"I thought you guys were bullying her that night," she says while Jewel is in the Doll Salon changing. "Seems like she could use a friend. Or two. Can she swim?"

Lily and I look at each other. Everybody can *swim*.

Tess gets out enough pool noodles for everybody. "Maybe she didn't go to swim classes. Maybe her family couldn't afford lessons."

When Jewel comes back out, Tess hands her a noodle. She takes it, so I can't tell if she can swim or not, I mean, not without saying, "Race you to the end of the pool." I don't think she can, but she can even make not-swimming sort of invisible. She's not shrieking and cannonballing off the diving board or anything, but she looks like she's having a good time. Sort of.

Later while we're watching a movie Jerome texts me. *Is she there? Is that why I can't come over?* He says he misses us. He says he loves us.

Our parents think ur 2 manly for sleepovers, I text back. Which is true. Dad says, "Doesn't a grade-eight boy have better things to do?" It was okay when Jerome was short but just over last Christmas holidays he grew an inch and he's still going.

He texts Lily, *Can I come just for a while?*

No, we're having a clothes swap.

I love clothes swaps.

You can't come. We'll be naked.

Me and Lily have a garbage bag each of clothes and shoes. Lily's clothes don't work for me because they're too small and scary, but I get a couple of good T-shirts of Tess's. I brought a dress that used to be Claire's, and Lily tries it on. It's so tight she looks like a hooker. She loves it.

Lily makes Jewel try on a whole lot of things, which is really the point. She fusses with Jewel's hair and wants to make a video of us on her phone.

"I don't want you to take pictures of me," says Jewel.

"Yeah, Lily, you can't do that." I make her stop. "You can't post it. Somebody might recognize Jewel."

"Nobody'll recognize her. Look at her!"

She's got on Tess's wedge sandals with Tess's old jeans. They're skinny but not so tight that everyone's going to be looking at her ass. She doesn't look anything like she used to. She looks taller. Older.

I hand her a big plaid shirt from my stuff. "Put that on."

Lily says, "No! No! That spoils it! Take it off!"

"Keep it on," I say to Jewel. "Lily's making you too pretty. People will notice you."

Jewel looks at me gratefully. "I can't take all this anyway. I don't have a place to keep it. It has to fit in my pack or my locker."

"You can keep it at the Doll Salon for now," Lily offers.

"With the rest of the doll clothes?" Jewel kind of smiles.

She made another joke!

Later, when we're in our sleeping bags, Lily asks Jewel about her little brother, how old he is and stuff like that. Jewel gets sad, but she answers. "He's five. I don't know what's happened to him since I left. I wish I could find out. I called the Children's Aid and left messages that they should check on him like six times."

"Why wouldn't he be okay?" I ask.

"Doesn't your mom look after him?" Lily asks. "I mean, she's his mom."

Jewel shakes her head. "She loses it when he starts screaming and hits him. Dad doesn't go near him. He calls him a cretin."

She says there's something wrong with Nico. "He was okay when he was a baby, but then he started to seem like he wasn't normal."

"Like how?" we ask.

"He didn't start talking. He's got sort of spidery looking, and he doesn't like anybody touching him. But you have to, you know, to get him dressed or give him a bath or change him, and then he cries. I read to him, but it's not like with Danny and Liam that I babysit. Danny and Liam lean against me when I read to them, or Liam sits on my lap. But Nico'll only lean against a cushion."

"He might be autistic," says Lily. "I have a cousin who's autistic."

Jewel nods like she knows what that means. I've heard of autistic, but that's all.

Lily says, "My cousin wouldn't play peek-a-boo or wave goodbye or do stuff like that."

"Nico too," Jewel says.

"Wouldn't Anton look after Nico, now you're gone?" Lily asks. Lily still has a bit of a crush on Anton, I think.

"Anton doesn't look after anybody except himself. It was Charmaine who was really good with Nico. She could get him to do things. After she went, there was only me."

"Where did Charmaine go?" I ask her.

"I don't know. One night I woke up and heard a lot of shouting and noise going on. Next day when I got up, Charmaine wasn't there. They said she ran away."

"Did they tell the police she was missing?"

She shakes her head again.

What a family. It's like they have some big huge secret nobody can know about.

"Do you have any pictures of your sister?" Lily asks.

She has a little one, in her wallet. She gets it out and shows us. "A friend of my mom's took it when we moved away from Montreal. I stole it."

It's a bunch of people lined up in front of a van. Six altogether, adults and kids, some smiling, some not. The big guy — he must be Jewel's dad — is good-looking in a tough kind of way, ponytail and beard, black T-shirt and leather vest and boots. Jewel's mom is all over him like a rash. She's dressed way too young for a mother, cleavage, short jean skirt, skinny legs, platform sandals. Big curly hair, big eyes.

"Your mom looks like a Barbie!" Lily screeches. Not tactful.

Jewel bites her lip.

The kid standing next to their mom must be Anton, shorter than now, dark hair and eyes like the mom.

"Aaaww," Lily coos. "Wasn't he adorable?"

And you can see he knows it.

Next in the lineup are two girls, one obviously Jewel because she's more or less invisible. You can't see her eyes because she's looking down. If I didn't know her and you took the picture away and asked me to describe her, no way I could.

The other girl is older and holding a baby. Its mouth is open, bawling its head off.

"That's Charmaine, with Nico," Jewel says.

And we go "Oh!"

124

Because Charmaine's not invisible. Light brown hair, shoulder length, dressed ordinary in a long-sleeve shirt and jeans. But really pretty. And smiling like she's sure everything is going to be better in the new place they're going to.

She's not even in the same movie as her parents.

"She's beautiful!" Lily cries. "How old is she?"

Jewel thinks. "Um, I was eleven when we moved here, so Charmaine would have been sixteen."

"Why doesn't she let you know where she is?" I ask. "Now you have her cell, she could call it and your parents wouldn't know."

"She doesn't know I have her cell. She probably thinks it's still under the bed. Or she might think they have it — my parents."

"But she could write to you. Send a postcard at least."

"Yeah, she sent me a letter once. Only I never got it. My parents saw it first and didn't tell me. The only reason I even knew was I found the envelope with my name on it, ripped up in the garbage. Just the envelope, not the letter. And in the same garbage I found where my mother wrote down an address in Belleville. That's why I went there on the bus, looking for her. For Charmaine."

So that must have been last year, when we heard about her running away the first time.

"I went to the address my mother wrote down, only Charmaine wasn't there. Another lady lived there, and she never heard of any Charmaine. I showed her the envelope and she said it was like months old. Charmaine might have written other times and my parents could have got those letters too. I'm afraid —"

"Afraid what?"

"I'm afraid my parents went looking for her like I did. Only they might have found her."

"But if they did, then you'd know," I say.

"Maybe not."

"What do you mean?" Maybe not, because they wouldn't tell Jewel? Because they don't want Jewel or anybody to know? What does she think happened?

She just shakes her head.

Lily tries to cheer her up. "Maybe Charmaine has a boyfriend she's living with. He wouldn't want her to go home."

"She had a boyfriend, Sam. My parents didn't like him. His family lived on a reserve. They made her break up with him."

"How old would Charmaine be now?" Lily asks.

"Eighteen."

"Well, *eighteen*. Charmaine can date anybody she wants now."

But I'm thinking if I was Jewel's sister, I'd try a lot harder to tell her where I was. To let Jewel know she was okay. Supposing she was okay, that is.

I'd find a way. If I didn't want my parents to know, I'd text my sister's friends.

But then, Jewel didn't have any friends.

If Charmaine still lived around here, she could come to the school and ask the secretary to get Jewel out of class to talk to her. Or she could leave her number with the secretary so Jewel could text her.

So I guess Charmaine doesn't live near here anymore. It's funny she only tried that once, though, writing that letter. I hope nothing happened to her. Nothing bad, I mean.

Next morning Jewel walks with me from Lily's back to my house. On the way I ask her again why she can't work something out with those people she babysits for.

"Couldn't you tell them you aren't getting along so well with your parents, and could you stay with them and look after their kids all the time? Wouldn't they like that?"

Jewel shakes her head. "I don't want to give them the idea anything's wrong. They might call the CAS or the police. They'd make me go back home."

"But you've got to go back *sometime.*"

"No. Not ever."

She's pretty clear about that.

"Well, you have to have some plan." She won't talk to the school counselor because she says Mr. Puddicombe would tell her parents. It all comes back to her parents. She gets fierce and trembly if we try to get her to talk about them.

"What about foster care?" I try.

She just shakes her head.

Well, okay. I knew this one girl, Kaylie, living in care. Two boys where she was living were hitting on her all the time, and when she told her foster mom, she got told she should learn not to be a tattletale. Finally she was moved and had to go to another school. After that I never saw her again.

"So …" I hold up my hand and count on my fingers. "You can't stay with the Owens. And no foster care. You can't stay in the school once the holidays start. And you can't have sleepovers with us forever, or stay in the Doll Salon."

"I could run away again."

I stop walking. "No, Jewel!"

She sort of smiles. "I don't really mean that. I got no place to go. I just wish I could have some place of my own. Some place my parents wouldn't find me."

"Like that cabin."

"Yeah, only where nobody would throw me out if they caught me. Some place that was mine and I could buy food and not be hungry."

"Like the Doll Salon."

"But that's Lily's. She doesn't want me staying there, not really."

"So, like an apartment?"

She nods. "Yeah, only, how do you get an apartment when you're thirteen?"

Once we get to my house, Jewel heads off to wherever she goes when she isn't with us. I'll see her later because she's coming to my house for another sleepover tonight. I watch her turn the corner. I feel really bad for having a nice house and nice parents and a nice room.

An apartment would be great. Only, like she says, how do you get an apartment when you're thirteen years old?

I sit on our front steps for a while, trying to think. How much would an apartment cost? Like five hundred dollars a month? That's a problem. Jewel gets money from babysitting, but it wouldn't be nearly enough for an apartment.

We've got two thousand dollars in our doll account. A lot of that is Lily's and some is Jerome's. I could make more if I seriously wanted to. I could fix up a lot more dolls and sell them online. Like I'm a good rerooter. It's boring, but I can be fast if I want. Also, I get an allowance.

"What are you doing out here, Maya?" Mom just opened the front door. "I thought I heard voices earlier. Come in."

"I'm gonna go for a bike ride."

"Take Claire," she says, but I say I'm not going very far and run to get my bike from the garage before she can stop me. "Have you got your phone?" she calls.

Of course I have my phone. I head in the direction of our school, which is also the direction of the university. The students left a month ago, but there's still plenty of places with For Rent signs outside. One is two blocks from our school. Somebody's painted the porch the university colors — red, yellow and blue. It doesn't look that great. There's a dozen recycling boxes on the front walk with soggy flyers in them.

How much can it cost to rent a dump like this?

I drop my bike on the lawn, or where the lawn would be if there was any grass, and ring the buzzer.

No answer. Maybe the buzzer doesn't work. But I put my ear to the door and hear buzzing. I ring some more.

After a long time, I hear footsteps. The door opens and a guy is standing there in boxer shorts, flabby hairy belly, smelling like beer and sweat.

I almost say, "Sorry, wrong address," but I make myself ask if the apartment's rented and how much is it.

"We're not taking ten-year-olds." There's pillow lint stuck to the stubbly whiskers on his face. He scratches his belly and starts to shut the door.

"It's not for me. Anyway, I'm sixteen."

"And I'm Peter Pan." He shuts the door. I hear the lock turn. Creep.

I don't exactly know why I do what I do next. By now I'm on the side of town where Jewel's parents live and suddenly this idea comes into my head that I want to see their house. I know the name of the street, Merton, because Jewel must have said it once. Another time I remember she said it was three blocks from where she babysat.

I figure it'll have to be the worst-looking place on the street, no lawn and junk spread around. But when I get to Merton Street, none of the yards look near as bad as that Peter Pan guy's place. It's not a very long street and I bike up and down it a couple of times and don't have a clue what place belongs to Jewel's family.

I'm just about to give up when a motorcycle thunders around the corner and blasts past me. It pulls into a drive with a couple of old vans parked in it and a chain-link fence at the back. The engine roars a couple of times and goes silent. I only got a glimpse of a helmet and leather jacket going by me, but I think it might be Jewel's dad. Or Eddie.

The house is ordinary looking, white, a porch across the whole front with a couple of plastic chairs. I get off my bike across the street and pretend like I'm having a problem with my chain. Meanwhile I have a good look through my spokes.

I remember that time Jewel showed us a picture of her family, and I can imagine her mom in the kitchen, wearing sweats and smoking and drinking coffee. Her dad coming in the side door and getting a beer out of the fridge. Anton, probably taking another shower. And Nico — does Nico ever get to have a shower? Does anybody take him outside to play? Jewel said she used to take him to the park. He loved going on the swings and he cried when she stopped pushing.

I'm crouching over my bike thinking all this stuff when the front door opens. A guy steps out on the porch and flicks a cigarette onto the grass. I know from Jewel's picture that no way it's her sort-of-hunky dad. This guy is short and mostly bald, with a ponytail.

Eddie.

The corners of his mouth go up and his tongue comes out and licks his lips. Like I'm seeing him in close-up slow motion. Lizard tongue licking his lips.

He's smiling right at me. I swear his tongue has a fork in it.

The door opens again and another guy comes out, a bigger guy. Eddie turns and says something and then they're both standing there staring at me.

I drop my head and jiggle my chain some more.

Then, nice and slow, I wipe my hands on my shorts and get back on my bike and push off.

Once I get around the corner I start going like a bat out of hell. I don't stop until I'm home. I prop my bike against

132

the house and have to lean against the wall until I get my breath back.

I text Lily and say I need her to meet me at the Tea Shop. We get our usual booth, and I tell her about seeing Jewel's house and Jewel's dad and Eddie. I tell her about Eddie licking his lips at me.

She makes a face. "Eww, gross. Sorry, Maya. What's her dad like? Scary?"

"Well, big, anyway. You know, tall and built like a bull-dozer."

"Why did you go around there anyway? What if Anton looked out and noticed you?"

He sure never noticed me when I was a nerdy grade six kid.

"I was just biking around." And I explain how I started out looking for an apartment for Jewel.

Lily snorts. "Uh, Maya, kids can't rent apartments."

"Uh, Lily, I know that." I tell her about the Peter Pan guy. "He was almost as bad as Eddie. The place was disgusting. Jewel couldn't live there."

"It'd probably be cheap, though. How's she supposed to pay for an apartment?"

I take a deep breath to start my pitch.

And then Lily totally blows me away. "We have all that doll money. I got three hundred for that last doll I did."

Wow. I thought she'd be a lot harder sell. "I thought you were saving to start a business."

She brushes it off. "We're not even in high school."

"What about Jerome?" He won't like us giving our money away.

"I'll handle Jerome."

Also, if we get Jewel an apartment, she's out of the Doll Salon.

Except then Lily says, "But Mom sees my PayPal account. She'll see the money going out and want to know what for." Lily's PayPal and Facebook and YouTube and Instagram are all hooked up to her mother's email account so her mother can see what she's doing.

"If my parents found out about any of this, Maya, Mom would cut off my accounts — my PayPal and eBay and all my doll sites."

I don't think Mrs. Larsen would really cut Lily off. I've heard her bragging to my mom about Lily and her doll business. But I don't push it. I never get that far pushing Lily anyway. I'm already pushing her about Jewel sleeping at the Doll Salon on Sunday nights.

And then she says, "But Jerome's parents never look at his PayPal."

"Right. Like Jerome's going to pay for an apartment for Jewel."

"I'm just saying, we can figure some way to do the money. Anyway, for a while." She gets out her phone and starts looking up apartments on Airbnb.

"It can't be anywhere that other people are living," I tell her. "If that Peter Pan guy thought I was ten, he'd think Jewel was eight. Also, we'd have to find somebody who looks old to rent it for us."

"I'm a good actor."

"You do old fantastic on the phone, Lily, but you do not look old in person."

"I could wear glasses."

"Yeah, right. And put talcum powder in your hair. And get a cane. What about your sister?" Tess is old. She's eighteen.

"Tess would *so* tell. She is *so* into rules."

What are we going to do then? Like stop somebody on the street and get them to rent an apartment? Like getting college kids to buy beer?

The Tea Shop door opens and a guy comes in. We look at him and at each other.

And then we call out, "Hey, Jerome! Over here!"

Jerome comes over, not exactly Mr. Friendly. He's not too happy about us not letting him hang out as much.

"You want to get some cake with us, Jerome?" I ask.

"Raspberry Death by Chocolate," he calls to Mr. Brunetti's niece behind the counter. "With four forks."

"Three forks," I say.

His eyes light up. "Clonella isn't coming?"

"Not today. It's only us."

He puts his bag on the floor beside Lily. "You dumped her?"

"She's got something else on."

"Huh." But he looks happy and goes to the counter to order his tea.

"How much are we allowed to tell him?" Lily hisses across the table.

"Nothing," I hiss back. "We promised."

"But we have to tell him the apartment's for her."

"Yeah, but definitely we don't tell him about her living in the school."

"We're going to live in the school?" Jerome is back again. "Like at Hogwarts?" He sits down with his tea and stirs it.

"That stuff smells like pig urine," Lily tells him.

"And you would know?"

"Jerome, can you make your voice lower?" I ask.

"You think I'm too loud?" He starts whispering. "Is this a secret meeting?"

"No, I mean lower like you're older." Jerome got kicked out of choir last year when his voice broke. "Like can you sound eighteen?"

"Sure." He growls in his Humphrey Bogart voice, "We don't need no stinking badges." And in his Monty Python cheese-shop voice, "Wensleydale? Stilton? Emmental? Cheddar?"

"Don't get him started," says Lily.

"Just do a normal eighteen-year-old guy voice," I say.

"Quick, gimme a beer, I'm dying," he croaks. Then he gets all suspicious. "What's this about, anyway?"

"We want you to rent an apartment." Lily passes him her phone with some listings she's bookmarked. "We need you to check these out."

He starts laughing like a hyena. "*Exactly* what I need. A cool apartment where I can invite all my friends." Then he frowns. "What's it about?"

"It's for Jewel," I say.

He laughs some more. "You're joking, right? You want me to rent an apartment for Clonella? How old is she? I mean, thirteen?" Then he looks around and whispers loudly, "Is this for something *illegal*?"

"Not exactly," I say. "She just needs a place to live."

"Uh, excuse me if this sounds dumb, but don't thirteen-year-old girls live with their parents?"

"Jewel doesn't have parents. And we can't tell you any more than that, Jerome, because it's very, very secret."

"And you are the one person we can trust to do this," says Lily. "Also, you look older than you really are."

He strokes his chin thoughtfully. Jerome is the only boy in our school with a soul patch, did I say?

"Hmm," he says in his Dracula voice. "Verrry interesting. Tellll me morrre."

We make him swear that he won't tell anybody and he swears. Then we tell him that Jewel is in a bad situation and urgently needs a place to live. It has to be a studio or bachelor apartment that's not too expensive but not horrible either. We want him to go and look at places for us and rent one as soon as possible.

"Say you're renting it for your older sister," Lily says.

Jerome nods. "Oh, yeah, my totally cool older sister Lucille. For when she gets back from Paris."

"It has to be somewhere nobody can get a good look at her," I say. "Because they'll know she's not old enough to live on her own. It has to be private. And nice. And safe."

"Single room with private entrance," Lily reads out. "That's on the Student Housing site. I thought you'd need student ID to go on it, but it let me in."

"Okay, send me the links. I guess I can try to look at them."

It's a deal. Jerome's already eaten half the cake himself.

"But not dressed like that," says Lily.

"What's wrong with how I'm dressed?" He looks down at his black hoodie and dirty cut-offs.

"You're dressed like a kid. You need to look like a university student."

"Like with a Queen's jacket? One of those purple ones?"

"Just a regular jacket?" I look over at Lily.

She nods. "A sports jacket, with a white shirt. And glasses. We can get a jacket at Goodwill. The dollar store has glasses."

"I feel like Ken," says Jerome.

"And not those running shoes," I say.

"It *could* be running shoes," says Lily. "Students wear shoes like those. Anyway, it has to be lace-ups, so we can put cardboard in the heels and make him taller."

We decide that Jerome will rent a cheap apartment for Jewel as soon as he can and then we can all take the bus after school to Value Village to buy stuff for it. We can tell our parents it's for the Doll Salon.

"I feel like Ken with bendy elbows," Jerome sighs. "Why isn't life always this much fun?"

4
How to Live in a School

Jewel

They treat me like I'm a doll. What happens when they get bored and want a new one? They have rich parents and big houses with enough bathrooms for everybody and no weird stains on the walls.

What happens when they decide I'm not good enough to be their friend?

Maya likes me most, I don't know why. Lily likes me but as somebody to fix up. She's afraid of getting in trouble if her parents find out she lets me stay in that dollhouse. I don't blame her. Her parents are nice, but my dad can be nice too when he wants. It's different when nobody else is watching.

Jerome doesn't like me. Maya says he's jealous, but that doesn't make sense. I think Jerome thinks I'm too low class.

It's weird living in the school and I liked the cabin better, but compared to sleeping outside, the school is not so bad. Only, it would be so easy to get caught. Also to get locked out, which I did. And it's not that comfortable.

The first night I was so tired I fell asleep on a bare metal shelf hiding in the supplies cupboard from Ms. Waldie and the custodian. When I woke up, I was so stiff I could hardly move. It was like my veins were squashed flat and my blood couldn't move around my body. I got my clothes out of my pack and spread them under me, and that was softer, but then I was cold and I had to put some of the clothes on to keep warm. I didn't sleep much the rest of the night.

Next day I had the idea of going to the Lost and Found and saying I lost my yoga mat, because a mat would be better to sleep on than the bare shelf. I knew they had lots of mats, because once I lost my pencil case and I went there to see if anybody found it, and I couldn't believe how many mats they had lined up against the wall. Nobody even bothered to go back for them. So at recess I went to the Lost and Found and said I lost my mat, and the two bossy grade six girls that run the Lost and Found asked me, "What color was it?" and I said blue because I could see blue ones. And they said "Which one?" and I said, "It doesn't matter."

But they made me look at them all. One had a corner torn off, so I said, "That's mine." I put it in my locker until the end of the day. It was better sleeping that night, and then I got the idea of buying a floaty mattress from the dollar store. I blow it up every night and put it under the yoga mat and it is quite comfy. Also at the dollar store I got a survival blanket that folds up very small.

The cabin was better than the school because of the trees and having a fire in the stove and melting snow and all that. It was only I got so hungry by the end. I couldn't have stayed there anyway, because sooner or later somebody would have come.

Or I would have got noticed, like when I was walking on the road into the cabin. I stood out, because nobody else was walking around.

At school I blend in, because at school it's all kids.

Teachers are a problem, though, because sometimes they stay late, especially the principal and the vice-principal, Ms. Harpell and Mr. Admunson. Sometimes they come back after supper for sports or music practices, or come in early in the mornings. There's cleaners too, but they don't do the art room and usually they're done by ten. The safest time to be out of the supplies cupboard is after that. Even then, though, some teacher could wake up in the middle of the night and remember they forgot something and get in their car and come in. Ms. Waldie would never do that. She's always the last teacher to get there in the morning. But I still have to be out of the art room before any other teachers show up and see me leaving.

I used to go out the main door when it was just getting light. Nobody was ever around to see me then. But then the locks got changed. I can go out okay but I can't lock the door after me. If I go out and leave it unlocked, somebody could notice and wonder what's going on. So what I do is, I go in the washroom and sit in a stall until I hear kids in the hall. It's boring and not too comfortable, but I read or do homework.

The hardest part of living in the school is I have to be careful every second that nobody sees me. I can do that, though. I guess I learned how at home. And in the school most people have more to think about than somebody they don't know, unless that person really stands out.

Downtown near Tim Hortons there's a man who sits on a bench in his old coat, even when it's summer, and he never

145

cuts his hair or his beard. People notice him. He must want to be noticed, because he sits in the middle of everything and yells. Once he yelled at me, which scared me a lot because usually nobody sees me.

Anyway, I'm not like him. I don't wear scary old clothes. I wear what the other kids wear. Not what Mom buys me — I don't like flashy or bright colors like pink or red. But she forgets, or she doesn't care. Maybe she thinks she'd like me better if I was dressed like somebody else. When I don't wear what she buys me, she gets mad. Once she got me cut-offs so short my butt hung out. Anton said I looked like a hoozey. I don't think that's actually a real word, but that's what he said. I don't like wearing shorts anyway, or dresses. My legs are too hairy.

Anton won't wear stuff she buys if he doesn't like it, and she doesn't get mad at him. He won't wear Goodwill if it's not a label. Last year he grew so fast I got lots of good stuff that was too small for him. Also, sometimes Mrs. Owen gives me things she doesn't want, like T-shirts. Mrs. Owen is nice most of the time, except if I do something to make problems for her. That makes her mad. Like if I'm late, I get a lecture. So I'm never late.

I knew when I came back from the cabin I was in for a big lecture. That's how she is, so I thought, okay, get it over with. Actually, I was surprised she let me come back. I was nervous walking over there, partly because somebody might see me, but none of them at home ever come down that street far as I know. The Royal Hotel and the smoke shop are the other way.

I felt weird ringing the bell at the Owens', everything looking exactly the same as when I left — kids' trikes and toys on the porch and the snow shovels still out. Nothing was any different except me. It seemed a lot longer than ten days that I'd been gone.

I didn't go in like usual, just rang the bell and waited. Mrs. Owen opened the door and the boys came running out, shouting "Jewel, Jewel!" and hugged me around the knees. Mrs. Owen made them go watch a DVD and told me to come in the kitchen.

I sat at the table and she stayed standing up, her arms folded.

"Why didn't you let me know you were going?" she asked me, very stern.

"I left a message."

"Only on the day you left. And why didn't you tell me when you were going to be back?"

Because when I went away, I wasn't planning on ever coming back.

I didn't say that. I just said I was really sorry, it was a family emergency and I didn't know when I'd be coming back.

"You have a phone. You could have called me. You made life extremely stressful for me and my family, Jewel. I had to find someone else at very short notice."

I said I was really sorry again and that my phone battery was dead and I forgot to take my charger.

She made her lips into a thin line. "When you're older and you get a job, your employers won't be very sympathetic if you just disappear. You won't have a job for very long." She

147

said more stuff about thinking about other people instead of only about yourself and about being responsible, but I knew she wouldn't keep on for too long because she always has things she has to do. I was pretty sure now she wasn't going to fire me.

And I was right, because pretty soon she said, "Well, Jewel, let's try to put this behind us. Can you stick the lasagna in the oven in an hour? I have to do some errands, but I'll be back by six." She took her keys out of her purse and rushed out.

I went in the living room, and the boys stopped watching their movie and looked up at me.

"Hey, what do you guys want to do? Play Lego? Read a story?"

Danny smiled then. "Lego first." We started making a big car garage.

After a while he said to me, "Are you going to go away again?"

"No, I hope not." I didn't like lying to him, but I didn't know what was going to happen and I just wanted him to be happy. "If I do go away, I'll always come back and see you."

Liam put his hand on my knee and said, "You went away." He's little, only four and a half.

And I said, "I'm really sorry, Liam." Because I know what it's like, not knowing. When Charmaine was just gone and nobody told me where she went or why, all I could think about was, when is she going to come back?

But I never thought Danny and Liam would care that much. They have their parents who love them and take care of them. They have a million toys. I felt bad if I made them upset. And that made me feel really bad for Nico, because he doesn't have me or Charmaine to love him and look after him now, and he doesn't know where we went or if we're ever coming back. For sure nobody will be telling him.

That made me feel so bad I had to put up a huge Stop-Thought in my mind. I called the Children's Aid six times and left a message. Tomorrow I'm gonna call and see if they went.

I stayed at the Owens' house until six-thirty and fed the boys their supper, and Mrs. Owen said I should come again the next day. I said okay and, just like that, things were back to normal.

Normal, except for I was living in the school.

Walking back there from babysitting, I started worrying if I could get in again. I worried the main door would be locked and Ms. Waldie's keys wouldn't open it. I was afraid somebody would see me trying to unlock the door. It wasn't even seven, and it was completely light.

When I came around the corner, I saw a couple of parents talking by the front steps. Then some kids came out the door and I slipped in before it shut again. It turned out it wasn't locked anyway.

There was a basketball practice on, balls banging and feet pounding up and down the gym. Upstairs was orchestra practice, violins squeaking and all that. The music room is along the hall from the art room, so I walked up like I was

149

going to music. I had my yoga mat tied on my pack and my floaty mattress and blanket, so I didn't need to go to my locker. If anybody was out in the hall, I would just walk down to the girls' washroom.

Nobody was in the hall. I went straight across and put my key in the lock. In two seconds I was inside with the door shut.

The good thing about living in the school is that eating is no problem. Not like at the cabin. At least, it's no problem if you have money, and I do from babysitting. The parents make the food in the cafeteria, so it's good for you. They sell pizza, but only healthy pizza, and no chips. Also, when I'm at the Owens', Mrs. Owen tells me to help myself to a snack, and when I give the boys supper, I can eat with them if I want.

Keeping clean is more of a problem. Our school doesn't have showers. When I'm at the Owens', if both Mr. and Mrs. Owen are out at the same time, I can wash my underwear or extra jeans there and throw them in the dryer while I have a quick shower — a really quick one, though. I can't wash my hair because Mr. and Mrs. Owen would notice it was wet. I have to wash my hair at school in the washroom sinks, and that nearly got me caught. Well, actually, it did get me caught.

It was a couple of weeks after I started living in the school. One morning I was really late getting going. My alarm went off okay, but it was so gloomy outside I accidentally went back to sleep. When I woke up again, it was almost seven! I ran down the stairs and put bread in the lunchroom toaster and ran back to the washroom. Even though it was so late, I really wanted to wash my hair, because it was gross. I gave it a quick wash in the basin and dried it under the hand dryer.

And when I stood up, two girls were standing there staring at me.

I had this weird flash they must be living in the school too. Which was stupid. I knew those girls, they were rich, they had good lives, they didn't have to run away. I didn't say a word, just grabbed my stuff and walked past them into the hall and downstairs out the main door.

It was raining but I hardly noticed. I was shaking all over. I forgot my toast in the lunchroom so I walked to McDonald's and got hot chocolate and a tea biscuit and sat there until I calmed down.

I felt sick about those girls seeing me. And angry. What business did they have being in the school that early? They must have been there for music or something, but why so early? Then I remembered I knew one of them — Maya. She was my lab partner in shared science with the other grade seven class. She and that other girl were best friends. Maya was nice, though. Not stuck up like the other one.

That's what I thought then. I had this idea of what Lily was like. It was wrong, because Lily isn't stuck up, she's almost as nice as Maya. It's just because of how pretty she is and the clothes she wears that I thought she was rich and stuck up. I heard Trevor Slick and Ben Neva call her a skank, but they're ignorant. They think that about her because of

151

how she dresses. Anyway, I know Lily now, and she isn't any skank. The only boy she talks to is Jerome, and Jerome doesn't like her that way.

But I didn't really know Lily or Maya then and I was sure they'd tell on me. I was so upset, because it meant I would have to run away again. Only, it was raining and where was I going to go? Eventually I calmed down a bit and told myself, okay, but all they know is I was at school really early, same as them. They don't know about the art-room cupboard. If they asked me what I was doing drying my hair in the washroom, I'd say my parents dropped me at school early because they were going to Montreal and my hair got wet waiting outside.

I mean, if my hair got wet from me standing outside in the rain, why shouldn't I dry it in the washroom? The school was open. It's my school too. It wasn't like I was hurting anybody.

I saw them at shared PE and they didn't say anything. Maya smiled, though, and that worried me. All I could do was wait and see what happened.

The thing was, nothing did. Not until later, anyway, and that was coincidence, Lily and Maya seeing me again that night I got locked out. That was a good thing, I guess. It was a good thing because I didn't know where I was going to go.

Living in the school is not like having a home. You can't go there when you want — just when nobody will notice. On the weekends now I can't stay there, because my keys don't work anymore so I'm locked out. Usually I go downtown, walking around like I'm a tourist and hoping nobody from school shows up. I blend in, especially since Lily cut my hair and gave me clothes. I wear sunglasses I got at the dollar store.

One day I'm walking along behind a family — a nice ordinary mother and father and two little girls. Not too close but close enough for somebody to think I could be a sister trailing a bit behind. We come to an ice-cream place, and the little girls start yelling they want ice cream.

I'm standing there reading the board with all the flavors on it when the doors open and a guy and a girl come out. They're holding the biggest cones I ever saw, laughing and licking to keep the ice cream from dripping down their arms.

It's Anton. My brother.

I walk off slowly the other way. My ears are buzzing and black specks are whirling in my eyes. I don't turn my head to look again but it was my brother for sure, with a sharp haircut and black T-shirt and shorts. I never saw the girl before. I turn up at the next corner and keep on going. I don't look behind until I'm at the lights.

Nobody's following me. Anton didn't even see me.

But it was close.

5
Caught

Maya

After Lily and Jerome and I are done at the Tea Shop talking about apartments, Lily's sister picks her up. I text Mom to say I'm biking home. Jerome watches me unlock my bike from the rack.

"Hey, Maya," he says. "Tell me again why Jewel needs an apartment?"

We never did tell him in the first place, actually. "It's private. Jewel's business."

"Okay, so then … why I am supposed to help?"

"So you can get a cool jacket and glasses?"

He shakes his hair out of his eyes. Maybe his hair's too long for somebody to rent him an apartment. Maybe Lily should cut it.

"Why should I help if you won't trust me?" He gets a sly look on his face. "It's something to do with Lily thinking that Jewel was living in the school, isn't it?"

I forgot he knew about us seeing Jewel drying her hair in the washroom.

"Don't be crazy. You and Lily followed her after school, and she went home."

"But she didn't really live there, did she? I'm right, aren't I? She's living in the school?"

He keeps on about it until I get tired of listening to him. "Shut up, okay?"

"Ha! She is, I can tell! Cool! How does she do it?" Like he might want to try it himself.

I didn't tell him. He guessed it. I make him swear a hundred times he won't say a word to anybody, and he goes all indignant. "Do I look like a blabbermouth?"

No, but he's not too good with boundaries. Also, half the time he lives on another planet.

I start walking, pushing my bike, and he walks along with me, asking more questions. And I do tell him a bit, now that he's guessed it. I tell him how Jewel found Ms. Waldie's keys, so she could get in the school any time until they changed the locks. How she sleeps in the art-room cupboard and makes toast in the lunchroom and washes her hair in the girls' washroom. And he keeps saying, "Cool!"

Then he says, "But why's she living in the school? Why doesn't she go home?"

"That's her business."

He rolls his eyes. "Oh, right. Why tell me? I'm a guy, I don't have *feelings*. I can't *empathize* like a girl. And I have such a perfect life myself."

Jerome doesn't say much about his life. All I know is, he and parents can't be in the same room for five minutes before somebody starts yelling. I end up telling him how Jewel's parents beat up her and her little brother.

"They're not allowed to do that," he interrupts. "She needs to tell Mr. Puddicombe."

"Yeah, well, try telling her that. She's scared of what her parents will do if she tells. She says they'll kill her for running away and she can't ever go back. She called Children's Aid on them about her little brother. She's petrified they'll find her. Her older sister ran away a year ago, and Jewel's never heard what happened to her. She's afraid it's something really bad."

"How do you know she's not making it up?"

"She's not." I tell him about going to Jewel's house and seeing Eddie and Jewel's scary dad. I shiver even telling about it. "That's one reason she left. This Eddie guy was coming in her room. And her folks knew, and he's still their friend! He's still hanging around their house!"

Jerome narrows his eyes. "Does Lily know all this? And she didn't tell me?"

"We promised Jewel we would never tell. And neither can you. Anyone. You swore."

"But what about the little brother? Doesn't he need to be rescued from those guys?"

"Well, there's a mother. And Jewel's brother, Anton. Remember Anton? He was at our school last year."

"Oh, yeah. Anton. Thought he was a big dude." Jerome thinks for a minute. "You went to look at their house? Did Jewel tell you where it was?"

"No, I found it myself."

"What street?"

I tell him. Maybe I brag a bit about figuring out it was the right place from seeing Jewel's dad turn in on his motorbike and Eddie coming out on the porch.

"He creeped me out, looking at me. Like he could see me in my underwear."

"Eew."

I jab him with my elbow.

He yelps. "I don't mean eew, you in your underwear. I meant him looking at you like that."

We stop at the end of my drive. "You can't ever tell anybody I told you, remember," I say. "I shouldn't have said anything."

"But why not?"

"Because it's not my stuff to tell. And because I'm afraid you'll tell."

"I won't!" He looks insulted. "Who am I going to tell anyway? I don't have any friends except you and Lily."

He walks off down the street and I can practically see a cloud of question marks like flies buzzing around his head. I wish I'd never said anything to him.

When I text Lily, she says it's okay that I told him Jewel is living in the school since he already guessed it. She says we need Jerome to help us find an apartment, so it's fair he knows why. She's been lining up some places for him to go and see.

That night the sleepover is at my house. Me and Lily and Jewel and Claire eat pizza and watch a movie. It's a long one. It's still not over and it's almost eleven when I hear the phone ringing upstairs.

Mom comes down and pauses the movie. We all yell.

"Sorry, girls, but that's Jerome's mother on the phone," she says. "Have you heard from Jerome lately? His parents don't know where he is. They're worried he's not answering his phone."

We hardly ever know where Jerome is. He hasn't texted, though. Lily texts him but he doesn't get right back to her. She calls and gets the usual message saying his mailbox isn't activated. She shrugs. "Weird."

"Probably he left his phone somewhere," I say. But I'm getting a bad feeling.

Mom goes back upstairs and we go back to watching the movie. Just when the credits start to roll, the doorbell rings. I hear Dad go to the door.

Voices. Jerome's.

Lily and I run upstairs. Right away I see something's happened. Jerome's hair is hanging all over his face and he has a raw red scrape on his jaw.

"Are you all right, Jerome?" Dad asks.

"Yeah. I fell off a curb."

"Was someone harassing you? Bullying you? Have you been in a fight?"

"No, I just tripped. I'm a klutz."

"Your parents are very worried that you're not answering your phone," Mom says. "You'd better call them right now."

"My phone's broken. Can I use yours?"

After he talks to his parents, he comes downstairs with us and drops onto an empty piece of couch. "I'm getting picked up in ten minutes. They're freaking out."

Mom is coming down the steps again.

"Mom," I say, "we want to talk to Jerome for a minute." I look over at Claire. "Alone, okay?"

She hesitates. "Five minutes," she says. "Come on, Claire, time you were in bed." She goes back upstairs and Claire stomps up after her.

"So what happened?" Lily asks Jerome.

"Something bad." He swallows. "Something stupid." He looks over at Jewel. "I went to her house."

"My house!" Jewel jerks straight up on the couch. "Why? Why did you go there?" She looks from him to me and Lily. "You *told* him!"

I admit it. "It's my fault."

"No, it's not," says Lily. "It's nobody's fault. Jerome guessed. Jewel. Let him tell us, okay?"

And Jerome tells us what happened.

After he walked back with me from the Tea Shop, he kept thinking about what I told him. He got this idea in his head he'd go find Jewel's house like I did, and see if he could see Jewel's dad and Eddie. Maybe he'd see something illegal going on, like drugs or something. Maybe he could see Nico.

Once it got dark, he walked to Jewel's street and found the house from what I told him about the porch and the vans in the drive and the chain-link fence. He sneaked in behind the vans to try to look in the kitchen window. He saw people moving around inside, heard voices. He moved closer to try to hear what they were saying.

All of a sudden the security lights blazed on.

"What the hell do you think you're doing here, creep?" somebody yelled. A hand grabbed the back of his jacket and jerked him around, shoving him against the wall. It was Anton.

Jewel's dad came out the back door with scumbag Eddie. "What the fuggin hell's going on out here?"

"This kid was trying to see in our window," Anton yelled.

Jewel's dad grabbed the front of Jerome's shirt and lifted him right off his feet, stuck his face right in Jerome's. The smell of booze coming off him practically singed Jerome's eyebrows.

"What the hell you looking for, kid?"

"Little bastard was trying to steal a bike," says Eddie.

Jerome fumbled for his phone, thinking he could dial 911 without them seeing.

"You playing pocket billiards, kid? Let's see what you got there."

"My phone!"

Jewel's dad grabbed it. "Didn't really think a weenie like you would be carrying a knife. Nice phone. Too bad it don't work." And he lobbed Jerome's phone over the vans out to the street. Jerome heard it hit the pavement.

"What's a little fag like this want with a bike, Eddie? It's something else he's after. I figure he's gonna tell us what."

"Want me to lean on him a bit?" Eddie took hold of Jerome's arm and twisted it up behind his back.

All this time Anton was just standing there. "Dad —" He was looking freaked. "Dad, I know him. He knows who I am. He goes to my old school. Jewel's school."

Jewel's dad stared into Jerome's face. "No shit," he said. "Loosen off on that arm a bit, Eddie."

And then they asked him what he knew about Jewel.

Jewel is on her feet, her face totally white. "You told them! You told them where I was!"

"I never did!" Jerome yells back. "I never told them a thing! I said I didn't even know you. I said you're only in grade seven and I'm in grade eight."

"They made you tell them!"

"They didn't." He stops and takes a deep breath. "But I would have, if they really tried to make me." He covers his face with his hands and his shoulders start shaking. His voice comes out muffled. "I would have. I would have told them anything."

Jewel draws back into the corner of the sofa, staring.

Lily puts her arms around Jerome. "But you said you didn't tell. Anton stopped them, right?"

"Yeah." After a while he straightens up and wipes his face on his sleeve. "I guess he thought they'd be in trouble if they broke my arm." He sniffs and tries to laugh. "They'd have to kill me. But they didn't really think I knew anything. They just thought I was some little weenie snooping around."

"So they let you go?" I say.

"Her dad dragged me out to the street and gave me a kick in the ass. I fell down and they all laughed and went back in the house." He takes his phone out of his jeans. "Look at this thing. I found it in the street. It's screwed." The plastic is crunched in at the top and half the glass is missing. He looks like he's going to cry again.

"You can get a new one," Lily says. "We'll pay for it out of the doll account."

I get Jerome a Coke out of the bar fridge and half of it goes down in one swallow. He still looks awful and his face is bleeding a bit. I get him a Kleenex.

"I'm really sorry," he tells Jewel. "I don't know why I thought it was a good idea to go over there. But I never let on I knew you."

"Did you see Nico? A little kid?" Her voice is low.

"No, only Anton. I didn't go in the house."

She nods. "Okay. Don't *anybody* go near my house ever again."

Jewel takes off in the morning before anybody else is up. She's supposed to be coming for supper at Lily's but she texts us she won't be there but can she stay over in the Doll Salon. I know she's upset about last night. I try to get her to meet up, but she's turned off her phone and I don't hear anything from her all day.

Before I go to bed, I text Lily to ask if Jewel turned up. She texts back *im not going out 2 look.*

Next morning a crack of thunder wakes me up that's so loud I think it's a nuclear explosion. It almost knocks me out of bed. I hear Mom and Dad running around shutting windows. My clock says 6:05, but it's dark outside. I pull the covers up to my ears and try to get back to sleep.

Next thing I know, Mom's standing beside my bed shouting. "Maya, wake up!"

I open one eye. She's wearing her Cruella de Vil face.

"You've got some explaining to do, young woman."

Seems that Lily's dad just called. He went out to check to see if the roof was leaking in the Doll Salon and found a girl sleeping on the couch.

"Who was it?" I ask.

"I think you know."

"Did he catch her?"

"No."

"Then why —"

"Just get dressed, Maya. We're going over there."

When Lily's dad opens the door, I can see Lily in the living room. She's in a T-shirt and jeans, no make-up. Her eyes are red. She's jammed between Mrs. Larsen and Tess on the couch. Tess nods at me, not exactly friendly.

"I only saw a head sticking out of the sleeping bag," Mr. Larsen tells Mom. "I didn't want to scare her, and I figured Lily would have some answers, so I came in the house and got her. Couldn't have taken more than three minutes, tops. And when we get back out, it's like nobody was ever there. Not a thing out of place. I look in the little bathroom. Nothing. I look under the table behind the couch. Then I put my hand on the couch. And the cushions are still warm."

Jewel must have lit out of there in ten seconds flat. Lily's dad finally found the sleeping bag stuffed in the beer fridge.

"You're sure it was Anna sleeping in the Doll Salon?" my mom asks. "You think she's run away from home?"

"It looks that way," says Lily's dad. "We're not getting a clear story out of Lily. We're hoping Maya can help us out."

"But that's terrible!" says Mom. "Anna seems like such a nice kid. Maybe not very happy, though. She's been over at our house a lot. Maybe that's a sign all's not well at home."

"She's at our place a lot too," says Lily's mom. "At least once a week. More often, even. She was supposed to come for supper last night, but she didn't make it."

Mom shakes her head. "When does she go home? It seems like she's with the girls most of the time."

Which is an exaggeration. It's mainly the weekends.

167

Lily's mom tut-tuts. "What's going on with her parents?"

"I've talked with the mother," my mom says. "Christina. She sounds pleasant enough."

"She seems a little flaky to me," says Lily's mom. "Stagey."

My mom folds her arms and looks at me and then Lily. "So what's the story, girls?"

It takes about four seconds and then Lily goes into meltdown.

"I told you, Maya," she wails. "I told you we shouldn't let her stay in the Doll Salon!"

They're all looking at me now.

"Let's have the truth, Maya," says Mom.

Lily's not doing eye contact. I take a deep breath.

"Okay, her name actually isn't Anna. It's Jewel. We're just helping her until she gets her life straightened out."

Lily's mom's eyebrows shoot way up. "Oh, really? How long has this been going on?"

And I start where the story started for us, when we surprised Jewel in the girls' washroom.

"Wait a minute," Mom interrupts. "You're saying this girl was *living* in the school? How did you work that out?"

"We saw her drying her hair in the girls' washroom really early in the morning," Lily says. "And smelled burnt toast. It wasn't even seven thirty. But then we forgot about it until we saw her outside Metro at night — at the start of June, the last PA day. Tess drove us to get Certo."

"Tess, you knew about this?" Mrs. Larsen asks.

"No! They didn't tell me anything."

"And what about Jerome, girls?" Mom asks. She starts getting excited. "Jerome is surely in on this too. He turned up on our doorstep on Saturday night in a terrible state. I'll bet —"

"Jerome's not involved," I say. It's not exactly a lie. Jerome didn't know hardly anything until Saturday. Two days doesn't count.

"We're getting sidetracked," says Mr. Larsen. "Why don't we let Maya tell us the story — without any interruptions?"

Mom glares at him.

I explain about figuring out Jewel didn't have anywhere to go when we saw her outside Metro. "She was living in the school, but the keys weren't working because the locks were changed. She got locked out."

I go through the whole story. What our parents get most upset about is that they didn't know about any of it.

"But we promised Jewel," I say.

"You couldn't trust your parents to figure out the right thing to do?" Mom cries.

"Jewel wouldn't let us tell. She made us promise. She was *terrified*. Something really, really bad is going on with her family. If they find out where she is, they could kill her."

"You're being melodramatic," Mom snaps. "I talked to Jewel's mother. I didn't get the impression she was any homicidal maniac."

"Uh, you talked to *Anna's* mother," Lily's dad points out. "And there isn't any Anna."

"But I have the number in my phone," says Mom.

"All right, girls, whose number is it?" Lily's mom asks us.

Mom is already calling it. She puts her phone on speaker. The message starts up.

"That's not the mother's voice," Mom says.

"It's Jewel's sister's message," I say. "It's Jewel's sister's phone. Charmaine's."

They're all looking really confused.

"So the sister was pretending to be the mother?" Mr. Larsen asks.

"No, Charmaine ran away too. Jewel has her phone. She doesn't know where Charmaine is."

"Then who on earth was Christina?" Lily's mom asks. "I talked to her too. Several times."

Mom grabs my arm and pulls me around to face her. "Who was Christina, Maya?"

I can't tell them.

Lily clears her throat. "It was me."

"You?" Lily's mom bursts out. "But I *talked* to her. I would have recognized my own daughter."

Lily smiles a bit. "I didn't *actually* talk to you, Mom. You left messages and I left messages back."

Lily's dad cuts in. "Okay, let me sum up and see if I've got this right. There is no real Anna. There is no real mother watching out for her. What we have is a thirteen-year-old child, Jewel, who's been missing from home for — when did you say she left, Maya?

"March."

He shakes his head. "For … getting on to three months. *Three months?*"

Lily and I nod.

"And as far as we know, in all that time her parents have not reported her missing. Not to any of the authorities. Not to the school. Meanwhile, the child is sleeping in the school art-room cupboard. I find it hard to believe that's even possible."

"And what's she surviving on?" Mom cries. "Eating out of garbage cans? This is unbelievable! Insane!"

"She has money to buy food," I say.

"I suppose you girls are giving it to her."

"No, she babysits." I tell about the Owens. "Jewel can take showers there and wash her clothes."

"And we've been feeding her," Mr. Larsen points out. "She's been rotating between our houses. We've been giving a homeless child a bed when she can't get into the school to sleep in a cupboard. We're all involved in this."

"We need to call the police," says Mrs. Larsen. She's the lawyer.

I stand up. "But we can't —"

"Sit down, Maya," Mom says. "It's not your decision."

Lily's dad turns on the tennis on TV and puts on a pot of coffee. Everybody watches the ball on the screen go back and forth. At least it calms the adults down. Tess is allowed to leave, but Lily and I can't even go up to Lily's room. I don't know if Lily would even want me to. I can't tell if she's speaking to me. We have to sit in the living room with our parents between us, like we're under arrest.

I feel sick. What if Jewel gets caught and they make her go home? What will her parents do to her?

If only Lily's dad stayed out of the Doll Salon like he was supposed to. We had a plan. We almost got Jewel an apartment. It could have worked.

The police take half an hour to get there. They tell us their names, which I forget right away. They both have shaved heads, so it's hard to tell them apart except one has a shinier head. Lily's dad gets them chairs.

"We haven't had any reports of a missing girl fitting the description," the bigger police guy says. "We do have a record of a Jewel Morante from a year and a half ago. February. Belleville police picked her up there at a Tim Hortons and returned her home. That was the end of it."

Not for Jewel it wasn't.

"You say she hasn't been living at home since March of this year?" says the shiny-head guy. "But she's been going to school? Then where has she been living?"

Mom gives me the elbow. "Maya?"

"In the school."

They stare at me. "In the school!"

"Yeah." I explain about Jewel finding the keys to the art room and the main door of the school. I don't say Ms. Waldie left them in the art-room door.

"She's also been sleeping at our homes," says Lily's mom. "Under a false name. We weren't aware that she was a runaway. We weren't aware of any of what was going on under our noses until an hour ago."

The police aren't too happy to find out me and Lily have been hiding Jewel for a whole month, and they let us know it.

"Don't be too hard on them," Lily's mother says sharply. "They're children."

"Children need to take responsibility for their actions," the non-shiny head says. "It doesn't begin at eighteen."

"We *were* taking responsibility," I point out. "We were looking out for Jewel. Nobody else was."

That doesn't go down too well.

"Part of taking responsibility is deciding when a situation is beyond your ability to resolve it," I get told by Mrs. Larsen. "And taking steps to inform those who can."

The police get down to business. "You girls are in touch with her. Text her and ask her where she is."

Mom looks at me. I get out my phone.

Where r u, I type in. *Come back*. I send it. I feel like a traitor. I'm leading Jewel into a trap.

I stare at the screen for a while. Nothing. Good.

The police want us to show them all her texts to us and all ours back. They write down stuff including our cell numbers.

"Has anyone besides the three of you been involved in hiding this girl?" the shorter police guy asks.

"Well, the people she babysits for," I tell them. "But they weren't like hiding her. They don't know she ran away. She wasn't staying over at their house or anything."

They take down the Owens' address.

"And Jerome?" Mr. Larsen asks us again. "Are you sure Jerome didn't know?"

"He didn't know," Lily and I say together.

"We saw him on Saturday night," my mom says. "He'd had some kind of an accident. But the girls maintain it had nothing to do with Jewel."

"Well, it sort of did," I admit. They'll probably find out anyway. "He was snooping around Jewel's house, and her brother and her dad caught him trying to look in the window and they beat him up."

That sets off a riot. I never told Mom and Dad any of that.

"Did he report it?" the police ask.

"No," I say. "It happens to him quite a lot."

They make us promise that if we hear anything from Jewel, anything at all, we'll let them and our parents know. *Immediately*. They say they're going to Jewel's house to talk to her parents.

By the time they're gone, Jewel still hasn't texted me back.

The party breaks up after the police leave, and Mom hustles me to the car. While she's lecturing me about trust and responsibility, I keep checking my phone. I'm thinking I should text Jewel that we told the police everything.

Mom puts out her hand. "Give me that."

"Now what have I done?"

"Don't get me started."

Too late. She's already started. And it's not fair! I didn't try to help Jewel because I wanted to get in trouble. I was just doing the best I could until we figured out what to do. I promised Jewel I wouldn't tell. The only bad thing I did was break my promise.

I tell Mom I'm too upset to go to school and she lets me stay home. It's the third-last day before the holidays and nobody is learning anything anyway. I'm not allowed to talk to Lily, but I still don't know if she's speaking to me.

I don't get my phone back until next morning in the car on the way to school. Mom has been checking it to see if Jewel has texted me back.

Still nothing from Jewel. I've got texts from Lily, though. So she's not so mad at me she's cut me off. She doesn't write much but she's sent me a link.

"Mom! Mom!" I shove the phone in front of her. She pulls the car over to look.

Lily texted me a link to a news story. *LOCAL GIRLS MISSING*, it says.

There's a picture of Jewel's house with yellow tape around it.

According to neighbors, two girls in the family, Charmaine, 18, and Jewel, 13, have not been seen for some time.

"The story's out now," Mom says. "Are you still okay with going to school, Maya? You don't have to if it's going to be too upsetting."

"I'm okay. I'll go." I need to talk to Lily.

Soon as I'm inside, I head to the art room. The door is locked. It's early, so no sign of Ms. Waldie, no surprise. I knock on the door and listen. Nobody's down this end of the hall, so I knock harder.

"Jewel?" I say into the crack of the door. "It's me, Maya. Open up." I knock some more.

No answer.

The lump in my stomach gets worse.

When I get to my class, Lily isn't in her seat. Maybe she's staying home.

Everybody's looking at their phones and talking about Jewel. We're not supposed to have our phones turned on in school. I look at mine. There's the picture of Jewel's house with tape around it like for Halloween.

And then I find a new one: a bunch of guys with shovels digging up the backyard.

"Somebody must of killed her," Trevor Slick says.

"Cut her up with a chainsaw and buried the pieces in the yard," says Ben Neva.

I scroll down to an old school picture of Jewel. Long hair over her face, T-shirt with a stretched neck. Nobody'd recognize her now from it.

Mr. Bronson comes in and makes everybody sit down. He says he'll confiscate our phones if we don't turn them off and put them away.

"There's no reason to think anything bad has happened to Jewel," he tells us. "She's likely gone somewhere she feels safe. The police think she's frightened and hiding somewhere." He looks up and down the rows, catching everybody's eyes in turn. "Has anyone seen her since Monday?"

I saw her Sunday night. It's Tuesday morning. I shake my head along with everybody else.

"If you do see her, or if you have any information about her, you must let me or the office know right away. *Right away*. Is that clear?" Mr. Bronson looks straight at me, so I know the police got to him.

Lily slides in the door just as the bell goes. I scuttle back and try to talk to her, but Mr. Bronson tells me to sit back down in my own seat.

When the recess bell goes, I catch up to Lily. "Are you mad at me, Lil?"

"My privileges are cut off until I'm twenty-one, Maya." She glares. "I'm going to sue you." And then she laughs and hugs me. We go outside to check our phones.

Still no message from Jewel, but there's more stories online. One on the CTV site has a headline *GIRL, 13, LIVING IN SCHOOL*. It shows a video of a yellow digging machine in Jewel's backyard. The porch has the yellow police tape across it and a heap of flowers piled against the steps. At the front is a teddy bear with a red heart.

Jewel Morante, 13, has been missing from home since March. According to neighbors, an older sister, Charmaine Morante, 18, has not been seen for over a year.

I scroll down. It says Nico is in the hospital. *Suffering from physical injuries and extreme neglect.*

"What kind of psychopaths would do that to a little kid?" Lily shrieks.

Poor Jewel. She'll be really upset.

Just then Jerome walks out the main doors. The scrape on his jaw has turned into a big blue bruise.

"Guess I won't be getting that tweed jacket now," he says.

"At least you're not in trouble like us," I say. Lily already texted him that we told the police he didn't know anything before Saturday.

"You guys get all the glory. I don't even get my name in the paper."

"Our names aren't in the paper either."

"But everybody at school knows you're involved. Everybody knows you guys hung out with Jewel."

"It's not about your feelings," Lily tells him. "It's about Jewel. Where is she? Jewel's dad and Eddie might have got her."

Jerome looks stricken.

"No, they haven't, Lily!" I say. "She's just run away again!" She doesn't need to make it worse than it already is.

I read out where our school says Jewel's parents never let on she was missing.

School records indicate that the missing girl was absent between March 29 and April 8. A note signed by the girl's mother, Suzanne Morante, dated April 9, is in the girl's file. Says vice-principal Archibald Admunson, "After her return, she was at school every day. Her attendance was perfect from then on."

Lily is reading the same story off her phone. "Look, it says Anton is her brother. I don't think he's arrested or anything. Just his father."

"Good," Jerome says. "I hope they lose the key. I hope they arrested the other guy too. Scumbag Eddie."

The story says Mr. Morante is in jail, and Mrs. Morante is at some location known only to the police.

"It says Jewel's father was on parole, but he's back in prison because he broke conditions. Which was not to do anything criminal. For a start."

And at the end: *Police are concerned over the suspicious disappearance of an older daughter, Charmaine, aged 17 when last seen. School board records indicate she last attended high school more than 18 months ago. Her recent whereabouts are unknown. Police are not ruling out the possibility of foul play.*

Lily frowns. "What does it mean, *foul play*? Do they think Charmaine is dead? Is that why they're digging up the backyard? But she isn't dead, is she, Maya?"

"She could be," says Jerome.

"No, she's not!" I tell him how Jewel found a ripped-up envelope of a letter from Charmaine from Belleville.

Jerome shrugs. "So? Her parents could have gone to Belleville and killed her."

"Then why would they bury her in their backyard?" I say. "Nobody would be that dumb. They'd bury her in some woods where nobody would think of looking."

"Maybe they are that dumb," Jerome argues. "Maybe they went there and killed her but they didn't remember to bring a shovel, so they had to take her body home and bury her there."

"Stop talking that way!" I yell. "You're not funny, Jerome."

Lily holds her phone in front of my face with a picture of the flowers and stuffed animals and notes heaped on the porch steps.

"That is so tacky. It's like all those people are just *hoping* somebody's been killed."

"They're digging up the backyard for bodies," Jerome points out.

"Who says it's bodies?" I say. "They could be looking for something else."

"Like what? Drugs? Guns? Big bags of money?"

"News flash!" Lily waves her phone in my face again. "It says here the neighbors saw the police dig up a dead dog."

A dog? We all look at each other. A dog?

"That's just ... weird," Jerome says.

Then I remember Jewel told us once her family had a dog. A dog that killed Nico's kitten.

"Anyway," I say, "they're not going to be finding Jewel in the backyard. She'd go anywhere else in the world before she'd go home."

We're heading to our next class when Mrs. Krantz, the school secretary, comes pounding down the hall after us.

"Girls, the principal wants to see you in her office," she says. "Right away. I'll let your teacher know."

"What for?" I don't get an answer.

"What about me?" Jerome asks.

"You get to your class," Mrs. Krantz says. "The bell's gone."

"Guess I'm just a nobody," Jerome sighs and stomps off.

We don't even have to sit on the benches outside Ms. Harpell's office. Mrs. Krantz tells us to go straight in. Ms. Harpell is at her desk working on her laptop. She doesn't look up or say anything. We sit.

Ms. Harpell is sort of witchy-looking with a long nose and curly gray hair, but she wears really cool clothes and Jimmy Choo shoes. At assemblies and soccer and basketball games, if we're winning, she'll be cheering at the top of her lungs, happier than anybody.

Not today.

Her fingers tap her laptop. Lily is starting to hyperventilate. And then the door opens and Mr. Admunson, the vice-principal, comes in.

Ms. Harpell shuts down her laptop and looks at us over her glasses. Then she says in a steely voice, "So you both knew Jewel was living in the school and you didn't let anyone know. Is that right, Maya? Lily?"

We mumble yes.

"Do you realize that your actions have contributed to the seriousness of this situation? You knew Jewel was too frightened to go home, and you didn't tell anyone."

"We promised her we wouldn't," I say.

"Doing the right thing isn't about *not telling*, Maya," Ms. Harpell snaps. "This is about someone being seriously unsafe. Keeping a silly promise did nothing to change that for Jewel. Nothing to help resolve her trouble."

Lily starts snuffling.

"We didn't do *nothing*," I say. "We were looking after her. We helped her."

"You allowed a very dangerous situation to continue. To get worse. No child of thirteen should have to hide out in a school — in this school! And other lives were at risk. That little boy. You had a responsibility to inform your teachers and your parents about what you knew."

She goes on like that until she gets me crying too.

Mr. Admunson asks us a bunch of questions about how Jewel got into the school at night when it was locked. I don't want to get Ms. Waldie in trouble for being careless, so I just say Jewel found some keys.

"Do you have any idea where she might have gone?" Ms. Harpell asks.

We shake our heads.

"You're certain about that?"

We're certain. I wish we weren't. I checked for a text just when the bell went, and there wasn't one.

We get more third degree about what Jewel told us about her parents and if we knew about the notes she forged from her mother. We have to go over and over it about a hundred times.

I guess everything's out in the open now. Our way seemed like the best way, but I guess it wasn't.

When we finally get let out of the office, we're allowed to go to the washroom before we go to class. I see my red face in the mirror above the sink. I look awful. I splash cold water on my flaming cheeks.

Lily takes her hair out of its scrunchie and makes another messy bun. "That wasn't *so* bad."

Not so bad? She was like hyperventilating, even. She's not that good an actor.

"It was horrible, Lily! Ms. Harpell was so nasty and witchy, and Mr. Admunson was acting like Hitler."

"Oh, *Archie*," Lily says. "He's all huff and puff. So what do we do now?"

"Uh, we do *nothing*, Lily. Remember? We're not supposed to be doing anything *at all*."

Then she says, "I want to go look at Jewel's house."

"Why?" I don't get it. "What do you think you're going to see?"

"You and Jerome saw it. I just want to see it too."

"It's just an ordinary house. And we can't go. We're grounded, remember?"

"We can text our moms and say there's an extra rehearsal for the last-day concert."

"You're crazy, Lily. I'm not going near that place ever again. I'm not getting into more trouble."

But somehow, after school, Lily and I are walking over to Jewel's house so Lily can see it. I didn't like the look of it the first time and seeing it now makes me feel like throwing up. The front yard is all trampled and part of the big wire fence is down so the digger could get through, and there's police tape all over everything. A crowd of people are standing around trying to see what's happening in the back. Guys with shovels working back in the yard. Big piles of dirt everywhere.

"They should put in a swimming pool when they're done," some guy says. "The hole's in the perfect place."

"They found a dead dog," some lady says.

"Shot between the eyes," another guy says.

The flowers on the porch steps are heaped higher than we saw in the pictures. There's more teddy bears and heart balloons and notes. Lily walks over and reads some out.

Dear children my heart goes out to you.

Praying for you Jewel and Charmin.

"Omigod." She rolls her eyes. "Charmin! Like the toilet paper!"

"Come on, Lil, let's go," I say. "We're supposed to be at rehearsal."

We're heading back to school when Lily says, "The Owens' house is down the next block. Jerome and I followed Jewel there."

184

We stop in front of the house when we get to it. It's quite cute, with a bright blue door and big blue planters of blue pansies, and kids' toys and bikes on the porch.

"Let's ring the bell," Lily says.

"Jewel's not going to be here." The Owens would know about Jewel now, like everybody else.

"Somebody might be home, though. They might give us a clue where Jewel went." She rings the doorbell.

A lady answers the door. She's dressed like she's just got in from work, streaked blond hair, a bit overweight.

"Mrs. Owen?" we both say.

She looks us up and down — well, mostly Lily, who is wearing a pink ballet leotard with a polka-dot skirt and black ankle boots.

"I guess you're not selling Girl Guide cookies."

I say that we're friends of Jewel's.

"Friends?" She raises her eyebrows.

"We really are," I say. "She stayed at our houses."

"When she wasn't staying in the school?" Mrs. Owen glares at us.

"I guess she isn't babysitting today," Lily says.

"No. Considering everything, I wasn't expecting her." We look at each other a bit longer and then Mrs. Owen opens the door a little wider. "If you have something you want to say, you'd better come in."

We follow her down the hall. Going past the living room, I see two little boys in the middle of the biggest spread of Lego I ever saw. Danny and Liam. I wave at them and say hi.

The older one stands up and runs past me.

"Mommy!" he shouts. "Where's Jewel?"

"These girls haven't come to babysit you, Danny. They've come to talk to me. About Jewel." She takes him by the hand back to the living room and sticks a DVD in the machine. "You and Liam can watch your Spiderman movie while we talk."

He sticks out his bottom lip. "I want to talk too."

"No, Danny, it's grown-up talk."

Although we aren't exactly grown-ups.

We go in the kitchen and Mrs. Owen tells us to sit down at the table.

"Tell me your side of it, then," she says, not in the friend-liest tone.

"Why were you helping her hide in the school?" she goes on. "What made you think that was the right thing to do?"

"We told her she should tell the police or the school counselor, but that just made her more scared. She made us promise not to tell."

Mrs. Owen rolls her eyes. But she must be delusional if she didn't figure out herself something funny was going on. I mean, she never talked to Jewel's parents, and she knew Jewel was only thirteen. Not even that old when she took over babysitting from Charmaine.

"We were just wondering if you heard anything from her since Sunday morning," I say.

"The police asked me that too. I've texted her but she hasn't answered. I assume she's run away again. I don't suppose you know where to?"

We shake our heads.

"Did you notice that Jewel looked different lately?" Lily asks her.

She thinks about it. "She seemed to be taking more care with her appearance. I noticed that. I thought things might be a little better at home." She looks a bit guilty now. "The police thought I should have been more suspicious about what was going on in her life. But she was so good with the boys, always here on time. It was so handy. It was easier not to let myself wonder too much about her."

"Did you know she was showering here?" Lily asks. "She washed her clothes here too."

Mrs. Owen looks startled. "Now that you mention it, I noticed one time she looked damp. She said the boys had a water fight in the bath." She shakes her head. "I saw on TV that poor little boy being carried out of the house. He's just Liam's age."

She softens up enough to write down our cell numbers and give us hers.

"I'll contact you if I get any word from Jewel," she says. "Of course, I'll contact the police first. And if you hear from her, let me know. Tell her the boys are missing her. Tell her we're all missing her."

"That was a wasted trip," Lily says as we're walking away. "And she didn't even notice I cut Jewel's hair. I mean, honestly, adults. Is she like blind or what?"

187

Another whole day goes by and we don't hear from Jewel or anything about her. She knows we'll be worrying. Doesn't that matter to her? Or has something happened to her? It gets so I can't think about anything else. After school I bike around town looking for her.

Mom and Dad make me take Claire. We stop at Tim's and Subway and McDonald's. Also, we go in the library and look in all the corners.

On Thursday, school is over for the summer holidays. We have the big concert and the grade-eight kids get prizes and everybody gets out at lunchtime. When I get home, I want to look for Jewel again, but Claire wants to go to the mall to buy shorts and I have to go too. But, okay, the mall's a place I didn't think of. It's somewhere people hang out when they don't have anywhere else to go.

Claire takes about an hour trying on shorts at Garage. Mom keeps taking more pairs into the fitting room after the sales clerk gives up. I go outside, looking around.

A couple of kids from our class come by. Ralena and Lara, with Ralena's mom. I'm talking to them when all of a sudden I catch sight of a familiar hoodie.

"Excuse me a minute," I say and take off.

"Jewel!" I call, but she doesn't stop. I run and get close

enough to touch her shoulder. She gives a little scream and whips around.

It's not her. It's just some kid, ten or eleven. She glares, and so does the boy with her, her brother, I guess.

"Sorry," I say to the girl. "I thought you were somebody else."

"You scared the shit out of us," says the boy. I apologize some more.

Of course it's not Jewel. The kid I thought was her has long hair. Jewel doesn't have hair like that anymore.

By the time I get back to where Ralena and Lara were, they've gone. Claire has finally found the only pair of shorts in the world she can possibly wear, so we can go home. By now I'm totally depressed. Of course Jewel wouldn't be at the mall. The police probably look there for runaway kids all the time. They probably check the public library too, and Tim's and Subway and McDonald's.

We're almost home when I get a text from Lily. She and Jerome are working on dolls and I should come over.

I tell Mom that I don't think it's fair for Jerome and Lily to be at Lily's when I'm still grounded.

"Remember you have a lot more to be grounded about than Jerome does," she says. But she gives in and drops me off at Lily's. Maybe she feels sorry for me. Maybe she's sick of me hanging around moping. Anyway, I have to promise I won't go *anywhere* without permission.

In the Doll Salon Lily is putting a white lace garter belt and stockings on a Barbie repaint. Jerome is painting a full-body tattoo on a Ken doll. The design is navy blue and black, with swirls like ferns and hooks and feathers.

"It's Maori," he says. "I saw it on YouTube."

"It's beautiful." It really is. I pull up a stool at the counter to watch him.

"Too bad he wants to take Ken's head off and put a bird head on instead," Lily says.

"A real bird head?"

He nods. "A blackbird. Crow's too big."

I tell them I just thought I saw Jewel at the mall.

"She won't be around here anymore," Jerome says, not looking up.

"What do you mean? What are you, psychic?"

"Jewel's picture's all over Facebook."

"They're not supposed to put missing kids' pictures on the Internet," Lily says. "It's an old picture, though. Who's going to know it's her, the way she looks now?"

Jerome inks in a loop on Birdman's shoulder. "This town's still too small for her to be able to hide. She probably went to Toronto."

"What's she going to do in Toronto?" I say. "She's too young to get a place to stay. Or a job."

"She could go to a shelter."

"They'd turn her in to the police or the CAS." I dig out my phone again and look at it. Still nothing.

"She might have gone to Montreal," Lily says. "She used to live there, right? She told us about her gran there."

"Her gran lives in Quebec City."

"Well, maybe she's got a nice aunt in Montreal or somebody else she can stay with."

I'm looking at the little screen in my hand. Why won't Jewel text me? She knows how awful it is when someone goes missing.

Nothing happens on my phone, but all of a sudden this picture pops up in my head.

Jewel.

Beside a lake.

"What?" says Jerome.

I must have squeaked. Jewel beside a lake.

"I bet I know where she's gone. Back to that cabin in the woods."

"The police would have looked there already," Lily says.

"How would they know about it? We never told them."

"We didn't?" Lily frowns. "Maybe we didn't. But not on purpose. We just forgot."

"We need to go and take a look."

"How are we gonna get there?" Jerome asks. "It's too far to bike. And we don't know exactly where it is."

I don't remember asking him along. He's sticking pretty close to us since it all came out about Jewel. I guess because we held out on him before, he's making sure it doesn't happen again.

"Tess can drive us," Lily says. "She's just hanging around messaging her friends about how bored she is."

Tess is going to England in a couple of weeks, so she doesn't have a job or anything this summer. It's not like she's got anything better to do. But she's a harder sell than she used to be.

"You guys are supposed to be grounded."

"Not anymore," Lily says. "It's lifted."

Not for me. But I don't say anything.

"I'll have to ask Mom," Tess says. "And she'll say no."

"Aw, Tess," I plead, "do you have to ask?"

"It's not even an hour there and back, Tess," says Lily. "Just say you're taking us to the mall. Or the RioCan, to see a movie."

"Yeah," Jerome says. "*Parrot Vampires* is on."

"What if we find Jewel at the cabin?" Tess objects. "Everybody'll know I drove you."

"Then nobody'll mind," I say. "If we find her, they'll be really happy you drove us."

"Do you guys even know where the cabin is?"

She's weakening.

"It's on the way to the conservation area," I tell her. "Near where the school bus stopped on our trip and Marcia Harding threw up. Beside a lake. We looked it at through mica. I'll pay you twenty dollars for gas."

Lily types *Gould Lake Conservation Area* in Google Maps and shows Tess how far it is.

She sighs and puts out her hand. "Okay, Maya. Give me the twenty."

I text my mom to say Tess is taking us to a vampire movie at the RioCan. Mom texts back, *Will Tess be with you?* and I say yes and she says okay. Off we go.

It doesn't take too long to get to the turnoff for Gould Lake. The first few side roads don't look right to Lily or me.

Then we come around a corner and see water.

"There's the lake!" I yell.

Tess pulls over on the shoulder. Now I'm really getting excited. Across the bay is a log cabin with willow trees and a big wide porch with flowerpots on the front steps. Exactly like Jewel described it.

A woman in sunglasses is roaring around the lawn on a ride-on mower.

"It's the right road," I say. "It's not the right cabin, though. That's the one Jewel couldn't get in. We have to turn here and go all the way to the end of the road."

Tess turns in and drives past the log cabin. We pass four other cottages, one with cars parked outside. Then we come to a sign that says *No Exit*. Tess stops.

"We have to keep going," I say. "There's one more." I'm looking for a roof through the trees.

"If I break an axle, there goes your allowance for the next ten years," she says. "All of you."

We bump and sway along, and suddenly Jerome's head whips around. "Hey, did you see that? Back up, back up!"

Tess backs up. And there's the moose, just like Jewel told us, nailed to a tree. It is seriously creepy, with long strips of skin hanging off its face. The horns or whatever they're called must be six feet wide.

"Cool," Jerome breathes.

Tess starts up again. At the very end of the road is a cabin.

It has to be the one. It's a wreck, paint peeling off the walls, moss growing on the roof. No flowerpots, no lawn, no deck.

Tess turns the engine off and we get out. I check for footprints on the ground, but it's too dry and hard. I do see tire tracks, though. We walk up the path to the cabin and peer in through the window in the door. I see beer cans on a table.

It's the right place.

"Jewel?" I call out. "It's us, Maya and Lily and Tess."

"And Jerome," yells Jerome.

"Jewel! Jewel!" we all yell.

About ten seconds later a pickup truck comes lurching up the lane. It pulls in beside Tess's van and two guys climb out.

"You kids looking for somebody?" one of them says.

I go up to them. "This is your place, right?"

"Yeah." They're wearing sunglasses and baseball caps. I can't see their expressions, but they don't look that friendly.

"We weren't breaking in or anything." I'm trying to think of an excuse why we were doing the Peeping Tom act. But then I see they're not paying much attention. They're looking at Tess. They're like thirty, and she's eighteen, but okay.

Tess comes up and gives them a big shiny smile.

"Sorry about the trespassing, guys. We're looking for a lost girl. She ran away once before, and we think this is where she came. We thought she might have come back."

The way they look at each other, they know what Tess is talking about.

"No sign of her lately," says the one who was driving the truck. "We been here a couple of days."

"Since Sunday?" I ask.

"Sunday around suppertime. Me and Max both had vacation time owing. Thought we'd come up and wet a few lines."

On Monday morning, Jewel was still in the Doll Salon. "But she came here before, right?"

"Somebody did, yeah. But back in the early spring."

"Can I go in and check?" I ask.

They look at each other again and shrug.

"Pretty sure we would have noticed," the one who isn't Max says. "But be our guest, if it'll make you feel better."

They unload some boxes of beer out of the back of the truck. We follow them to the cottage. The door's not locked.

"We never lock it," Max says. "Somebody wants to break in, saves them smashing a window."

Lily and Tess and Jerome come in and go back out again. The place is kind of a dump. Jerome says he wants to look at the moose head. But I stay. I want to look around. The bedrooms have stuff piled all over on the beds and on the floor. The kitchen has the wallpaper Jewel described, with the little chickens and ducks. There's mouse poop on the counter and the stove. Jewel would have cleaned it up.

So she isn't here.

The guy who isn't Max is putting beer in the fridge. When I say thanks for letting me look around, he straightens and pushes his sunglasses up on his head.

"No problem. Hope you find your friend. Tell her she can come back anytime. When we came at Easter, it was like one of those extreme makeover things, eh, Max?"

"Unbelievable," Max says. "We messed it up a bit since, but not near as bad as it was. When you find your friend, tell her thanks."

I'm in a cold stone place, dead leaves and litter blown in the corners, empty bottles, cigarette ends. It's dark, but there must be light somewhere, because I see mist. Maybe my own breath. I hear my own breathing.

Or maybe not my breathing, that panting. Maybe somebody else's. Louder, louder. Nearer.

I scream and a hard hand clamps over my mouth and I can't breathe at all. I bite at the hand. I scream with all my strength. No sound comes out.

I wake myself up.

I'm still gasping when Mom turns on the light.

"Maya, honey, what is it?" She sits down on the edge of the bed and gathers me in her arms. "You were having a nightmare." Her hair falls around my face, and I lean into her warm-bed softness.

"I was dreaming. I thought I was Jewel." That horrible person in my dream, gagging me. It's like he's still here in the room.

She rubs my back. "Oh, sweetie. You're going to make yourself sick with this Jewel business. You have to let it go. The police will find her. That's their job."

Dad sticks his head in the door, blinking like an owl, his hair standing up like feathers.

"Everything okay in here?"

"Nightmare," Mom murmurs to him. "She was dreaming about Jewel."

Dad shakes his head and goes back to bed.

"But what if the police don't find her, Mom?" All the stories in the news about what happens to lost girls. We have to find Jewel before something happens to her.

"They'll find her." Mom says it like a promise.

I sit up and wipe my face on my sleep-shirt sleeve. "When they do, can she come and live with us? She can stay in the extra guest room downstairs. She doesn't need much space. She's used to living in a cupboard —"

Mom reaches for my hand and squeezes it. "Maya, I know you care very much about Jewel. She's a wonderful girl, I know that. But we can't just take a child away from her family. It's not that simple."

"Mom, she can't go back to her family. That's the whole point of *everything*." Doesn't she get what Jewel's life is like? After everything that's happened? I pull my hand away.

Mom hangs on and squeezes harder. "Sweetie, I'm sorry. It's the middle of the night and I have to work in the morning. We'll talk about it in daylight. Right now I want you to stop upsetting yourself and go back to sleep." She pulls the covers up to my neck, kisses me on the forehead and gets up. "And sleep in. That's an order. It's the summer holidays." She turns off the light. I hear the door softly close.

Summer holidays, yeah. Not much of a holiday for Jewel.

I lie on my back and try to work out what the dream means. That man with the choking hand. The dark place, the cracks and scratches on the walls. I try to bring them back into my mind.

Is the dream a clue? Is Jewel somewhere like that?

That horrible creepy man. I bite hard on the hand, feel it drop away. I try to see around me in the faint white light, make out the marks on the high stone walls. The dream is fading.

And next thing I know, it's bright daylight, almost nine-thirty. First day of the holidays. Fourth day Jewel's been gone.

Mom's already left for work. Dad is in his office talking on the phone, and Claire is at her friend's at a sleepover. I go downstairs and turn on cartoons.

I'm eating frozen mango slices out of the bag, wondering if it's too early to text Lily, when a text comes in.

I don't know what to do.

It's not from Lily.

I text back. *Where r u?*

No answer.

Jewel r u ok?

Still no answer. I wait a bit and text Lily. *Jewel texted!!!*

And right after, I get a text from Jewel. *Promise not to tell.*

Everybody said if I heard from Jewel, I had to tell. My parents, the principal, the police.

I text back. *I promise.*

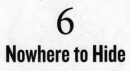

6
Nowhere to Hide

Jewel

When Lily's dad caught me sleeping in the doll house, I ran. I kept looking behind to see if he was following me. He wasn't, but I kept running. All I could think was how mad Lily and Maya would be at me for getting them in trouble.

It was raining and hardly anybody was on the street, but after a while I saw people looking at me so I slowed down. I wasn't running like I was going for a run. I was running like I was trying to get away from somebody.

I got to Tim's and changed in the washroom into my other hoodie and dried my hair with paper towels. Then I bought a tea and waited for the rain to stop.

For the rest of the day I mostly walked. The sun came out and it turned hot, so I went down to the waterfront where all the tour buses and tourists are, to blend in. I kept an eye out for Anton because of seeing him at the ice-cream shop that time. Mom and Dad never came to that fancy part of town, and Lily and Maya didn't either. Jerome, I wouldn't know where he went.

I followed people along the waterfront and went in all the museums where you don't have to pay. I kept my sunglasses on the whole time. I was glad now I let Lily cut my hair. Even my own brother didn't recognize me.

The whole day, all the time I was walking around, I tried to think of somewhere I could go. Not back to the school, even if I could still get in. Not to Maya or Lily's houses now. I'd an idea all along of going back to that cabin, only now it was summer and whoever the people were who owned it might be there. People would be at the other cottages too. They would think it was weird if they saw me there on my own. I might meet that Leora woman on the road again, and she wouldn't let me get away another time.

Also, I talked to Maya and Lily about that cabin. They'd have told everything by now.

While I was standing in line at another Tim's, thinking I'd get a sandwich wrap, all of a sudden the memory came back of the time at the Tim's in Belleville that the police caught me. That was just an accident. They weren't even looking for me. Now they actually could be. For sure Lily's dad would have called the police on me.

I got out of the line and bought a hotdog at the cart in front of city hall instead.

By then my legs were tired, so I went to the park and sat under a tree and read a book. I got it from a box nailed on a telephone pole, with a sign saying *Take One Leave One*. I took one but I didn't have one to leave, so thought I could just give the same book back after I finished with it.

The park felt safe, kids playing on the swings and slides, their voices all high and happy. Anybody who saw me might think I was some little kid's sister.

I wished I was there with Nico. I bet nobody was bringing him to any park now.

I sat and read the whole book. It was about a thirteen-year-old girl like me that everybody at her school thinks is a troublemaker. Her father disappeared and she and her friends rescue him by a tesseract. It's about good and evil and not getting sucked into the group mind. I liked it so much I went back to the start and read some of it again.

Then I walked around some more. I freaked out when I came around a corner and saw some cops walking toward me, but they turned out to be the kind that give out parking tickets.

I had a sort of idea I could sleep in a church, so whenever I came to one, I tried the doors. They were all locked, except one. That time there were people inside down at the front, talking. They turned around when I came in, and a lady asked if she could help me. I pretended I was looking at the colored glass windows and then I left, fast. Another church had a really old cemetery right in the middle of the city. Half of the stones had graffiti on them. There was a weird sort of stone shed with steps going down inside, and I went down the steps and had a look around. I thought maybe I could sleep on the pile of leaves that was in the corner. Then I saw an empty bottle and cigarette butts, and something under the leaves — an old sleeping bag. Or a person. I didn't bother finding out which.

Finally it started getting dark and I was really desperate. Ducking down a back lane, limping because I was so tired, I just hoped somebody'd left their garage door open. Nobody had. But parked along a fence was a dusty old car that didn't look like anybody'd driven it in a while. It wasn't locked.

The back seat had old mail and stuff piled on it, but I pushed it over and got in and locked the doors from the inside. If anybody came and tried to get in — like whoever owned the car — I'd deal with it.

That's what Dad always said. Deal with it. I hadn't thought of Dad in a while and I didn't want to start now. Stop-Thought.

And nobody came near all night, except for some raccoons.

Next day was more or less the same, walking around, getting something to eat, walking around, stopping to read when I got tired. But I wasn't as worried as the day before, because I thought I would be able to sleep in that car again, and I did.

The day after that, though, was a very bad day. I woke up with bites all over me, probably from the fleas of the dog or cat of whoever's car it was. And then, on my way to use the bathroom at city hall, I heard a terrible noise.

Motorcycles, roaring.

Right in front of city hall, hundreds of bikes were lined up, with more pulling in all the time. Harleys and Triumphs and BMWs, choppers and hogs, all polished up, the sun glinting on them blinding bright. The growling and revving made the inside of my skull shake. Every time a bike went past me, I stopped breathing. I remembered Lily saying that lots of them were just old guys and old ladies. But I felt like Dad was here somewhere.

He wasn't supposed to be here. The whole idea of us leaving Montreal and coming here was that nobody would know where he was. But I felt like any minute he would come around the corner.

Then I saw him.

Not Dad. Eddie. He was right across the street from me, big as life, with a red plastic cup of beer or something in his hand. Laughing and talking to some biker guys. He looked like he was having a great time. Back with the old gang.

Eddie.

Dad said the gang had people everywhere. He said no matter how hard I tried to get away from him, they'd find me.

I walked away fast. I went back to the park where the little kids were playing, all the time trying to calm down and catch my breath. But at the park there were big tents set up all over the place for the bikers. Bikers in leathers were walking around carrying their helmets. Some were speaking French.

Bikes kept roaring past me, going up and down the street, and I got it in my head it was Dad and Eddie and the gang looking for me. The first back alley I came to, I went down it. Somehow I ended up at the university, in a cafeteria. A lot of kids' camps were going on, kids running around with violins and canoe paddles. Nobody paid me any attention. I still couldn't calm down, though.

I couldn't wait for the day to be over. I couldn't wait to get back in that car, fleas and all, and pull my hoodie over my head.

Only, once the day was over and I got back to the car, a party was going on in the yard right beside it. Not bikers, just ordinary people, but a bunch of them were leaning against the car, drinking beer. Leaning against *my* car. I wanted to scream at them. I walked around the block, but every time I came back, they were still there.

No way I wanted to be out on the street now it was dark. Especially with motorcycles still roaring around. I went down by the lake and sat on the rocks by the shore. There was a couple of people kissing and laughing, but after a while they left. Then it was just a bunch of Canada geese settling down for the night, snorting and snuffling to each other, and I decided I'd just stay there. Mr. Bronson at school said coyotes ate Canada geese, but I didn't think coyotes came right in the city — not in the summer anyway.

I crawled under a park bench and rolled myself in a ball with my pack for a pillow. I thought I would be too scared to sleep, but I wasn't.

Only, later I woke up again, and it was only one o'clock. The ground was hard as the art-room cupboard, but with no yoga mat and no floaty mattress. I left all that at school. I was so cold I would have cuddled up to a goose in a flash if one would let me. I put on my other hoodie and wrapped my other jeans around my middle, but after that I didn't sleep hardly at all.

When it finally started getting light, I was stiff and sore and I had goose shit all over me.

I went back down to the shore and watched the sun come up. My teeth were chattering and it took ages to get warm. That was enough of sleeping outside for me. One night.

I was so sick of having no place to live. It was scary and tiring, but boring too. I couldn't babysit, I couldn't go to Maya's and watch a movie. I couldn't go to Lily's and watch her put new hair on a doll. I couldn't even take a shower. I had blisters on my heels.

I listened for motorcycles, but this early it was all quiet. When I walked downtown, I couldn't see a single bike. They'd vanished like they'd never even been there!

Dad and Eddie were still out there, though. And Mom. For sure by now the police told them I was still in town. Or Dad would have figured something out when he caught Jerome hanging around our drive. For sure they'd be looking for me now.

I was just fooling myself, hanging around. If it wasn't my family that saw me first, it would be somebody from school or something. Sooner or later, if I stayed around, somebody'd catch me.

I was right out of ideas. I didn't have any choice. I had to leave.

I caught a bus out to the station, feeling nervous going in because I was thinking the police might be watching for me, like they do on TV. Which was stupid, because why would they care that much about catching me, a kid? I wasn't some criminal. I thought of the time I wanted to go to Belleville to find Charmaine and being so worried they wouldn't let me buy a ticket because I was too young. I felt a lot older now.

Maybe I would go Toronto and look for Charmaine. I had some kind of feeling she might be there, because Belleville was partway to Toronto and she might have kept on going. But all I knew about Toronto was it was big, and that made me scared.

The board up on the station wall said the next bus leaving was for Montreal, so I got a ticket there instead. Montreal was big too, but I lived there once. It didn't really matter where I went, as long as it wasn't here.

In the washroom I scrubbed the goose shit off my jeans with paper towels. That still left time to get some coffee and yogurt and a cranberry-blueberry muffin, and by then the driver was letting people on the bus. I walked to the back and sat by the window and put my pack on the seat beside me. I hoped that would give people the idea not to sit down. I kept my sunglasses on and checked out everybody that got on the bus — nobody I recognized. Not very many people got on anyway, and nobody tried to sit beside me.

When the driver started up the bus and shut the doors, I finally let out my breath. Maybe I didn't know where I was going, but I was safe for now. Nobody in the world but me knew where I was.

I opened my coffee, which was still scalding hot. I meant to just eat the yogurt and save the muffin for later, but I ate it all. Seemed like I was really hungry.

The bus drove out to the highway past a bunch of gas stations and car lots and carpet stores. None of it was what you'd call nice looking, but all of a sudden I felt sad to be leaving. Right up until this minute all I'd been thinking about was getting away. Now I was wishing I could have said goodbye to Maya and Lily. All the time I was with them, I was worrying that I shouldn't be trusting them, thinking I had to keep them from taking me over. I thought they didn't believe how my life really was and they wouldn't be careful enough to keep quiet and they'd get me caught. That's how it worked out, but it wasn't their fault. I wanted to be inside their nice houses. I liked being looked after by their nice mothers and fathers. I could have got caught in the art-room cupboard at school too, and that would have been worse, because I probably wouldn't have got away.

Maya and Lily were just trying to help me. Maya especially, but Lily too. They knew they'd be in big trouble if they got caught. Well, now they were in trouble. I probably wouldn't ever see them again. They probably wouldn't ever want to see me. Maybe someday I would send them a post-card or something to say thanks.

Once the bus got on the highway, I started thinking about what I was going to do when the bus got to Montreal. I could speak French, but not as good as before. Once I got started again, though, it would probably come back okay. It was two years since we moved from Montreal, and I couldn't remember exactly where we used to live, except it was in Saint-Michel. I didn't remember anybody much from back then except for Mom's friend who took the picture of us the day we left. But if I went looking for her and found her, she'd tell Mom.

Hotels cost a lot of money, and a hotel wouldn't let me stay there on my own anyway. Maybe if I found a shelter, I could say I was sixteen.

Or maybe when the bus got to Montreal, I would just buy another ticket and keep on going to Quebec City. My gran lived in Quebec City. Gran liked me, and her and my parents didn't get on too well, so she might not tell. I might not be able to figure out where she lived, though. All I remembered was it was up the back stairs of a house. The time we visited her, Dad told us to go play outside, but it was raining. Charmaine and Anton and me sat on the back porch. We could see in the window of the house next door and their TV was on. All they watched was wrestling, but that was okay because we could see what was happening without any sound.

My gran cried when we left. "Tight old bitch," Dad said in the car. I guess he asked her for money and she wouldn't give him any. I guess that was the reason we came to see her.

I might be able to find her in the phone book, but she was old when we visited her the last time and she might be dead now. And going to Quebec would use up more money.

I had $237 in my account but that had to last me. Forever, maybe.

We stopped after an hour or so, and the driver said anybody who wanted had ten minutes to get a coffee in the restaurant or go to the washroom. But only ten minutes, or the bus would leave without them. Most people got off but I didn't. The bus had a washroom in the back, so I could use that if I had to.

I noticed the guy across the aisle from me had left a newspaper on his seat when he got off. Not that I would ordinarily have noticed it, only it had a picture of me staring up out of it.

I grabbed it and shoved it under my pack out of sight. It took a while to work up the nerve to pull it out and look at it again. At least then my heart stopped thumping quite so hard.

Nobody in the world would recognize me from that picture. I looked about eight, and ugly, really bad hair.

Then I saw the other pictures. One was our house, and one was somebody carrying something out the door in a blanket. For an awful moment I thought Nico was dead, but it said underneath he wasn't.

Then the driver came back on the bus and started letting people on again. I folded up the paper to put it back, but too late. The first guy that came down the aisle was the one from that seat.

I was scared he'd be mad but he said, "Go ahead, you keep it. I'm finished with it." He was Anglo, middle-aged, dressed nice. He sort of reminded me of Mr. Owen.

I said thanks and kept it. I pretended I was looking at my horoscope until he turned on his laptop. Once he wasn't paying me any attention, I turned away so he couldn't see the paper and looked at the pages with the story again.

It said Nico was in the hospital. That made me feel sick. I knew nobody would look after him properly and Mom would start knocking him around. Only it turned out he was in the hospital because Dad's dog Brandy went for him. Brandy was a horrible dog. Not a pit bull but he looked like one. He was always sticking his head in my crotch, and he killed Nico's kitten.

It was still my fault what happened to Nico. I didn't stay and look after him. I knew nobody else would.

So now I guess the whole world knew about our family. None of it was a secret anymore. The good part was, Dad was arrested. He was back inside. Mom was in a shelter. Why did she need to be in a shelter? Nobody ever did anything to her. She knew to stay out of Dad's way when he got loaded. It didn't say where Anton was, but Anton was never involved in Dad's stuff, at least that I knew of.

What I didn't get was why they were digging up our backyard. It didn't say in the newspaper, either. It said they found a dead dog, which would be Brandy, I hoped. But it still seemed like they thought something could be buried out there. Drugs, maybe, or money? It couldn't be me they were looking for, because they knew I wasn't dead. Eddie, I hoped. If they buried Eddie, that would be fine with me.

And then I had a sick thought that made me go cold all over. *Charmaine*. They were looking for Charmaine.

But Charmaine wasn't dead! I found that envelope with her writing on it. She got away from them, I know.

I tried to calm myself down, but I couldn't stay calm. Next I started thinking that if they didn't find anything in the backyard, if Charmaine was in Toronto or somewhere living her life, if Eddie was still walking around and not dead, they'd fill the hole in again and let Dad go. Nothing would be changed, except now everybody knew about my family and about me running away. I couldn't go back and hide in the school now. I couldn't babysit for the Owens ever. Maya and Lily couldn't hide me even if they still wanted. No way I could be invisible no matter how hard I tried.

I felt like I was going to throw up. I was so sick and tired, sick and tired of running away and hiding and trying to think what to do.

It wasn't fair. I was only thirteen. I leaned my forehead against the window and closed my eyes and tried not to cry.

"You okay there?"

It was the guy across the aisle, leaning toward me. I wiped my eyes on my arm.

"Yeah, I got allergies." I pulled some Kleenex out of my pocket and blew my nose.

"You sure you're not in any trouble?"

I shook my head and gave him a smile. "I'm going to visit my aunt in Montreal."

He was still looking at me. I was afraid he recognized me from the newspaper. He just read it too.

I got out my phone and turned it on and pretended I was checking it. After a while he shook his head and went back to looking at his screen.

Once I turned my phone on, about a thousand messages were coming into it. I couldn't believe it. All the time I couldn't even stand to look at that phone because it reminded me of Maya and Lily. I figured that would be the end with them. And Mrs. Owen, she got so mad the first time I took off, and this time I didn't even send her a text.

But messages were coming in from them all. From Mrs. Owen and the school and a whole bunch of other numbers

I didn't recognize. And from Maya and Lily and Jerome. But mostly from Maya.

I took a deep breath and read Maya's first.

She said I had to come back and that everything would be okay. Next message, the same. I don't know how many messages, she said it over and over. *Please,* she said. *Please, Jewel, answer.*

When the bus stopped again to pick somebody up, I went and told the driver I got a message from home that I had to go back because the aunt I was going to visit in Montreal was sick and my mother said to just come home. I didn't know if the driver saw the story in the paper. I didn't know if he might figure out who I was.

But he didn't act suspicious or anything. He said, "You're fine to get off here, young lady. You won't have a big wait. The bus coming from Montreal should be along in fifteen minutes. You got enough money for a return ticket?"

He told me how much it would cost, and I had plenty. I showed him.

"You can buy a new ticket from the driver. You might be able to get a refund for the rest of this one. Ask them back at the station."

I didn't care about a refund. I just wanted it to be over.

7
Lost and Found

Maya

Where r u? I text.

I'll be at the bus station.

Stay there!!! I'm coming!!!!

I text Mom I'm going for a bike ride and turn off my phone before she texts me to say take Claire. Claire's not back from her sleepover anyway. Dad's still talking on the phone in his office. I leave him a note on the kitchen counter.

It's a long way to the bus station, longer than I thought. Maybe eight or nine kilometers, heading right into the wind. It feels like I'll never get there and I'm terrified Jewel won't still be there when I do. That she won't wait. Or she's changed her mind.

My legs are killing me and my lungs are on fire. It feels like forever before I see the station at the bottom of the hill. I coast through the yellow light, lock my bike to a No Parking sign and tear inside.

She's not there.

Lots of other people are sitting in the chairs, standing around with suitcases, but none of them are Jewel. I go to the counter and ask what time the bus from Montreal got in and the lady says it isn't there yet! It won't come in for ten minutes. I have to go back outside and walk around until I calm down and stop sweating. I didn't bring any water. I

219

didn't bring money either, not even my debit card. Dumb!
Dumb!

Finally the bus comes. I go to the platform and watch a
bunch of people get off.

Not Jewel, though.

She tricked me.

And then she gets off. The very last person.

I hug her but she doesn't hug me back. I know I'm all
sweaty.

"Are you okay?" I'm talking in a low voice, like somebody
might hear us. Like we're secret agents.

She says yes, but she doesn't look okay. Her jeans and
hoodie aren't very clean and she's gray in the face.

"I got my bike here, Jewel. But let's go sit down a minute."
She follows me across the parking lot to a picnic table under
a scraggly tree. We sit.

"I know you didn't want us to tell anybody, Jewel, but
we had to. Lily's parents called the police. I'm really, really
sorry."

"That's okay." I don't think she means it, though. She
sounds so sad and flat.

"Your dad can't hurt you now, right? He's in jail." I don't
know if that's a good thing to tell her or not.

"But I don't have any place to go."

"You can come back to my house."

"No, not to your house." She shakes her head.

"Okay, then, the Tea Shop." That's where we went the very
first time she talked to us. "We can get something to eat and
figure everything out."

She screws up her forehead, like her brain isn't working fast enough.

"Okay," she says finally.

"I'll get Lily to meet us." She can bring money.

"Isn't Lily mad at me?"

"Of course not!"

"But I got you all in trouble."

"Not that bad trouble. It's not your fault."

I text Lily. I'm thinking I can ride my bike back to town and Jewel can take a bus or a cab, except I don't want to let her out of my sight. What if she disappears again? The city buses have racks on the front for bikes, but I don't have money for a bus.

"Can you ride my bike?" I ask her.

"Sure." But she doesn't sound sure.

"You can ride and I can run."

I unlock my bike and she gets on and rides in a little circle around the parking lot. She wobbles, but I don't know if it's because she's not a good rider or she's feeling wobbly. She says she's okay to do it, and I say, "It's not that far."

Well, it is far, actually, but that's how we get downtown. Well, I don't really run. We stop lots of times. It's even hotter now than when I came the other way, and my legs are already sore. It's a miracle we make it to the Tea Shop.

Inside it's like air-conditioned heaven. Lily's not here yet, so I have to tell Jewel I don't have any money.

"If you lend me some, I'll pay you right back. If you can't, that's okay. Lily will —"

"I got money. I can pay."

221

So we could have gone on the bus after all. I wasn't thinking straight.

We order tea from Mr. Brunetti's niece and ask for water. She brings two big glasses and we're gulping it down like we've crawled out of the desert when Lily bursts through the door.

"Jewel!" she shrieks and rushes over to hug her. I slide over in the booth to make room. My sweaty legs make a sucking sound on the seat.

Tess comes in right after Lily.

"She drove me," Lily says. "She was just parking." Jewel lets Tess hug her too.

"You don't need to be afraid of anything now," Lily tells Jewel. "Your dad's arrested, so he can't hurt you now."

She shakes her head. "But they think he killed Charmaine and he didn't. I know she's alive. They'll have to let him go again. They'll make me live with them again." She looks like she's going to be sick. "Eddie will still be there."

"Nobody's going to make you do anything," Tess tells Jewel in a voice like you use to stop somebody jumping off a building. "We won't let them."

Jewel swallows hard. "They were digging …" She can't finish it.

"I think the police thought there might be drugs buried in the yard," says Tess.

"Anyway, they didn't find any dead people," I say. "They found a dog."

"I know. Brandy," Jewel says. "I saw a newspaper that said he hurt Nico."

"It's all over the news," Lily says. "The police arrested a bunch of guys, not just your dad."

"He won't be getting out of jail anytime soon," Tess says. "He's been charged with drug possession and trafficking and breaking and entering. Violating probation. We saw it on TV."

Jewel sags in her seat. Then her face crumples up and her jaw starts trembling.

"I won't go live with Mom, I won't." She goes into meltdown. "They'll make me go into care."

Tess grabs our paper napkins and pushes them into Jewel's hand.

"I tried so *hard*," she wails. "For *nothing*."

"It wasn't for nothing," Lily and I tell her. "It's going to be okay, Jewel."

Mr. Brunetti's niece comes over with a box of Kleenex. Jewel keeps on crying.

"Sweetie, you know you couldn't go on living like you were," says Tess. "Foster care might not be so bad. It's not for your whole life."

"At least you'd have a safe place to sleep," Lily tells Jewel. "Better than an art-room cupboard."

"And you could still be at school with us," I say. "You could still babysit, even. Mrs. Owen wants you to come back. We saw her. She said to tell you they miss you."

"And you could still come to our places for sleepovers," Lily says. "It wouldn't be so different from before, except you could have your real name. Just be normal."

Jewel wipes her eyes on a napkin.

"What did you say about Mrs. Owen?" she asks me in a shaky voice.

Lily pushes the Kleenex box against Jewel's hand. "Me and Maya went to see her. She said they all want you to come back. The boys don't want any other babysitter except you."

"I thought she'd have had it with me this time. I didn't let her know I was going again." She sniffs.

"Why don't we all go back to our house?" Tess says. "Jewel, you can get cleaned up and have a rest and eat some lunch. And then see how you feel. We have to call the police and tell them you're safe, but not until you're ready."

Jewel puts her head in her hands. At first I think she's still crying, but she sits up and her eyes are dry. She was thinking.

"Don't call until I see my brother," she says. "I need to see Nico first."

The bell on the Tea Shop door jingles and we look over and there's Jerome.

"Oh, right," he says, hands on his hips. "Jewel's back, and look what happens. You're all having a party *again* and you didn't invite me."

He comes over to our table.

"Just kidding," he says. He's still got the big bruise down the side of his face. His mouth goes kind of funny. "Jewel, I didn't ever know how brave you are."

Tess drives us all to the hospital, including Jerome. He says no way he's not coming to *everything* with us from now on.

Tess goes to park the van, and we go in to the main desk. Jewel tells them, "I'm here to see my brother. His name is Nico Morante."

A lady at the desk looks at a list on the computer. She gets on the phone and turns away from us so we can't hear what she's saying, but she keeps looking back at us. I'm terrified she's going to say Jewel can't see her brother because he's dead.

Finally she writes something on a slip of paper and hands it to Jewel.

"Davies Wing," she says. "Seventh floor."

Jewel looks at the piece of paper like it's some kind of magic token. As soon as Tess comes in from parking, we all get in the elevator. Jewel is crammed in behind a guy in a wheelchair. Her face is white and set.

When we come out at the seventh-floor nursing station, she holds out the paper with the room number and tells them she's here to see her brother. The nurses go off to one side and talk.

There's a problem. There's too many of us. Yeah, like Jerome. And Tess. And me and Lily.

"You're his sister?" one of the nurses asks Jewel.

"Yes."

He explains that Nico can't have a lot of visitors at one time because it would be upsetting for him.

"Just me?" Jewel says. She looks scared.

"Well, maybe one other."

Lily gives me a little push. "You go, Maya." Lily is a good person.

The nurse tells them they can wait in the lounge, so that's what they decide to do. Then he says to me and Jewel, "Follow me."

We walk after him down the hall, our shoes squeaking really loud on the shiny tiles. We don't say anything. Every room we go past, I see little kids lying in cribs looking really sick. I get a picture in my mind of Nico with tubes coming out of him everywhere.

The nurse stops and says to Jewel. "Here's your brother's room." The sign beside the door has four names. One is Nicolas Delos Morante.

In the first crib a little girl with curly white hair is leaning on the rail, sucking her thumb. A little boy is asleep in the next one, and in the third there's another kid just lying there looking at us. The only other crib is empty.

So which kid is Nico?

Jewel is running back out of the room after the nurse. "My brother's not here!"

My heart starts thumping. This is too weird.

"Oh? Maybe they've gone to the sunroom."

They?

"He had a couple of visitors earlier," the nurse says. "I'll take you."

We go down another hall and stop outside a big room, very bright sun coming in the big windows. It's so bright it's hard to see.

"There they are. Your family."

Jewel takes a step back and bumps into me. I feel her ready to run.

Her family? Is her mother here? But I don't see anyone who could be Jewel's mother. I see a couple of little kids and some moms and dads and lots of toys and books. Over in the corner is one little boy all by himself, lining up toy trucks. A little boy in blue penguin pajamas, with one arm in a cast.

"Nico!" Jewel says in a hoarse voice. The little kid looks up. His eyes go scared in his skinny face. Dark circles under them and a big crusty scab on his cheek. His mouth opens to let out a wail.

"It's okay, Nico," Jewel says.

And at the exact same time somebody sitting by the window says the same thing.

8
Everybody Knows

Jewel

"It's okay, Nico," somebody says. The sun is in my eyes so I only see an outline, but I know the voice.

And I shout, "Charmaine!" and she's flying toward me and grabbing me and it's her.

My sister.

Nico is screaming his head off, and after a while Charmaine lets go of me to crouch down so her face is next to his.

"Look who it is, Nico," she says. Her face is all wet. "It's Jewel. Jewel!"

Nico keeps on for a couple more yells, but all of a sudden he stops. He still has his mouth open, trying to get his breath.

"It's Jewel, Nico," Charmaine says again.

Nico stares at me.

"Jewel," he says in a croaky little voice I don't even recognize.

I never heard him say my name before.

The nurse decides we need to go in another room where we can be private. It's not a very big room and there's me and Maya and Charmaine and Nico, and Charmaine's boyfriend, Sam. Sam brings Nico's trucks with us to the other visiting room. Nico sits on the floor with the trucks.

I sit on the other couch next to my sister, and she puts her arm around me. I feel a bit shy because I haven't seen her for such a long time and she doesn't look how she used to. She's skinnier and her hair is shorter. She looks older.

"Oh, Jewel," she says and starts to cry again. "I'm so ashamed of leaving you on your own. I knew awful things would happen. And they did."

"I ran away too," I say. "I left Nico, same as you did."

Charmaine tells me what happened to her. She doesn't exactly say it, but stuff was going on for her with Eddie like was going on with me. She told Dad she was telling the police if they wouldn't make him stop, and Dad called her a liar and a whore. Then he really started in on her and gave her a bloody nose. She got away from him and ran out the door without her coat or her purse or cell. She ran downtown to Starbucks, and they let her use their phone. Sam was in Belleville then, and he got in his truck and came and got her.

"I tried to phone you, Jewel," she says. "I called when I thought you'd be home, only you were never the one to answer. Usually I got Mom or Eddie and I hung up. One time Mom said, 'I know it's you, Charmaine. Don't call here anymore or he'll come after you.' I wrote you a letter. I hoped you'd get it before anybody else saw it. I guess you never did. They must have got to it before you did."

"I saw the envelope." I tell her how I came looking for her.

"Her dad did too," says Sam. "He saw the postmark."

"I was so stupid," says Charmaine. "Dad came to Belleville and started asking around. He knew Sam worked in construction. Somebody told him where we lived. When we got home, the people downstairs from us said some guys tried to get them to let them in the building. I knew it was Dad and Eddie. We packed up the same night and drove down east, to New Brunswick. Sam got another job and Dad never found us."

"I told her not to write or call anymore," says Sam.

"I should have tried harder," Charmaine says.

I take her hand. My sister's hand. I thought I would never touch it again.

"That's okay," I say. "I know how it is."

She wipes her eyes. "I called your school a couple of months ago, Jewel." She reaches her other hand out to Sam. "I didn't tell you, Sam. I didn't have to, because it didn't work out." She looks back at Jewel. "They said you were in Montreal."

I tell her and Sam I wasn't in Montreal, I ran away and stayed in that cabin in the woods. I tell them how I came back when my food ran out and then I lived in the school. And that Maya and Lily figured it out and helped me. And then I had to run away again.

"What if I never saw the story on the news?" Charmaine cries. "What if you never saw that newspaper on the bus?"

"But we did."

Just then somebody knocks at the door. It's Lily and Tess and Jerome.

"Maya, we have to go," Lily says.

"And you have to call the police, Jewel," Tess says. "You promised. That was the deal."

"I will," I say.

And Charmaine says, "I'll see that she does."

Maya stands up. "Jewel, if you need a place to stay —"

And Charmaine says, "Thanks, but she's coming home with me. Me and Sam are staying in Belleville, at Sam's parent's."

Maya's looking at me. It's like I can see inside her head. She's happy for me, happy I found my sister and brother, but she's sad too. She thinks now I'm done with her. Now I don't need her anymore.

But I'm not done. Maya is my friend. She saved me. She and Lily both, they saved me.

9
After

Maya

We're playing some game Lily got for Christmas, cards with questions on them. You have to turn up the card off the top of the pack and guess how the person next to you would answer. I guess the point of it is to see how well you know what your friends think.

So the question I turn up is *WHAT IS HOME? THE PLACE WHERE …*

"Where you keep your clothes and dolls," I say for Lily.

She rolls her eyes and holds up what she wrote. *Where my family is.*

"I was just joking." That's what I wrote too.

Then it's Lily's turn to guess what Jewel wrote. All of a sudden Lily doesn't look too comfortable.

Where your parents like some scumbag sex pervert better than you?

Where the dog tries to kill your little brother?

"Uh … Where nobody tries to make you into somebody you aren't?" Lily guesses.

"Pretty good," Jewel says. She shows us her paper. *Where I'm safe.*

"Where the refrigerator lives," says Jerome. "That's what I wrote." He leans back on his chair to get another Coke from the Doll Salon fridge.

"You're supposed to wait until Jewel guesses, Jerome," Lily tells him. "You're not playing properly."

He flicks his hair out of his eyes. "Because it's a dumb game with nosy little cards."

I'm with Jerome. What business is it of anybody's what *home* means to Jewel?

Of course she wouldn't say *home* means *family*. Not that family doesn't matter to her. She's a million times happier now that she's got Charmaine and Nico back. But all the rest of them — way too complicated. No wonder she doesn't mind living in care too much. It's probably the safest place she's ever lived. The foster parents are kind to her, and she has her own room and it's a hundred times better than an art-room cupboard.

Also, she can see Nico anytime she wants. He's in care too, with people who know how to help kids with the kinds of problems he has. He's doing okay.

Jewel says when Charmaine and Sam move back from New Brunswick, they might all live together. But maybe not. If Charmaine and Sam move back to Belleville, Jewel says she wouldn't like not knowing anybody at whatever school she'd be going to there. Here she can visit Nico, and she has friends (us), and she can babysit for the Owens. She says she'll see how things are going by high school, but she wants to stay here at least to the end of grade eight. She's working really hard and taking extra math because she says she wants to be an engineer so she can build her own house for her and Nico.

She still comes for sleepovers at our houses, but not so often. And we still do dolls in the Doll Salon, including Jerome, even though he's in grade nine. Lily says he's making a name for himself as a doll artist. So is Lily, of course. I actually don't like dolls as much as I used to, though I try not to let on. I feel a bit sad when they get all fixed up, with their smudgy eyebrows sharp again and shiny new hair where their old chewed hair used to be. I don't see why they all have to be perfect.

Besides, there's more interesting stuff to do besides dolls. A family just moved to our neighborhood that had such a terrible life where they came from that they had to leave with practically nothing, not even winter coats. Our school is having cookie sales and concerts and car washes to raise money to help them start over. One of the girls, Sahar, is in our class, and our teacher asked me and Jewel to be friends with her and show her how to do things. Sahar's English is not too great yet, but what she's told us about how she got here and what her life was like before would make your hair stand on end.

Most everybody I know lives in their own little world, but there's other stuff going on out there. You can't stay in some perfect little bubble all the time. I know you can't fix everything that's wrong with the world, but you can pay attention.

You can do that much, at least.

Acknowledgments

Unlike Jewel, the main character of *Almost Invisible*, I've been very lucky in the family I was born into. The wonderful settings my parents provided for us to grow up in show up in everything I've written.

When I was around Jewel's age, I had an elaborate fantasy of running away (from school, mostly) to our summer cottage and holing up there in winter, hiding my presence from anyone who came looking. I've used that fantasy by sending Jewel there (although our cottage is a little tidier). Jewel's hiding place in school also had its beginnings in my life, in a school art-room cupboard at Victoria School. At the end of June when nothing much else was going on, the art teacher asked me and my friends to help clean out the supply cupboard. The long deep shelves were stacked with abandoned student art and mysterious objects. The bottom shelf stored the huge six-foot rolls of paper our teacher cut into pieces for us to paint or draw on. We found that by scrambling over the rolls and stretching out behind them, we could completely disappear. That cupboard too came in very handy for Jewel.

Many people have helped to raise this book. George Lovell pushed me to finish it and racked his brains over the title. Leila Garvie gave me her unfailingly astute feedback. Mary Beaty, Johanne Pulker, Ellie Barton, Martina Hardwick, Margaret Bissell, Bonnie Thompson and Annie Conboy kept me on the right track.

Sara Marshall of Spokane, Washington, read the manuscript during a visit to Ontario in 2015 and told me I had work to do on the ending. Thanks to Bob Marshall, old friend, for introducing us.

My Tuesday-evening writing group at Queen's Ban Righ Centre, especially Kris Andrychuk, Bill Hutchinson, Jan Miller and Darryl Berger, responded invaluably to several versions in 1,500-word instalments. I'm grateful also to Lori Vos, Susan Mockler and Rebecca Gowan, the wonderful Stillpoint retreat group in Burnstown, for their encouragement, and to Sister Pat and Sister Betty for their hospitality.

And if it weren't for the amazing Susan Korba, I would know very little about the world of dolls.

Thanks, finally, to all the fine people at Groundwood and my great gratitude to the late Sheila Barry. One of the great pleasures of seeing this story make its way into print has been the opportunity to work again with Shelley Tanaka.

Maureen Garvie is a former teacher, journalist and librarian who now works as an editor for McGill-Queen's University Press. She is the author of three books for young readers, including *George Johnson's War*, co-written with Mary Beaty, *Lake Rules* and *Amy by Any Other Name*. Maureen now lives in Kingston on the shores of the St. Lawrence, in the same house where she grew up.